THE GAY
ILLUSION

by Duane L. Ostler

ISBN-13: 978-1542832748

ISBN-10: 1542832748

TABLE OF CONTENTS

This book is dedicated to:

the victims.

CHAPTER ONE

As John opened the door of the fast food joint, he was hit with a blast of sounds and smells that would have made even a hungry truck driver feel woozy. The stench of grease was mixed with the odor of sweat, onions, sweat, chili pepper, sweat and sizzling meat. Shouts and catcalls filled the air, mostly coming from the unfortunate employees whose every moment spent working in this fast food joint was a living torture. Between their shouts was a rumble of sound caused by the nonstop talking of dozens of patrons scattered in booths and at tables. They were chomping away on food that was only slightly less toxic than the nicotine the surgeon general warned about on every cigarette package.

John's eyes swam for a moment as his nostrils and stomach adjusted to the place. Why had Dr. Chester requested they meet HERE, of all places? When John had made the appointment with the famous shrink, he had expected to come to a cushy office and rest comfortably on a padded couch while pouring out his soul to a little man taking furious notes on a pad. Instead, the doctor's receptionist had instructed him to come here, to the "Wilted Chicken" fast food joint, where the food was as stale as the patrons.

Glancing around the room, John frowned as his eyes rested on beefy truck drivers, leather jacketed bikers, grizzled old men and a scattering of women who either looked embarrassed at being there, or were as fearsome in appearance as the men, and just as heavily tattooed. What respectable shrink would have a new client meet him HERE for a first consultation? What insanity was this, anyway?

To make matters worse, John had no idea what the good doctor even looked like. All the receptionist had told him over the phone was that "Dr. Chester will find you, so you don't need to worry. He will greet you as soon as you come in." Well, John was in, but he had not been greeted, even by a curious stare from anyone. He was being completely ignored by all of the patrons who continued to guzzle down "food" that was sure to give them indigestion before they even left the place.

"John Sanders, I presume?" said a sudden voice to John's left. Looking sharply around, John saw a large, obese man, seated at a booth next to the door. On the table in front of him was a splash of French fries and onion rings, as well as a partially eaten burger that looked rather green. The man sported a grey-white mustache and a goatee, which stood out in stark contrast to his nearly bald, shiny scalp.

The big man waved an arm toward the boy. "Come have a seat, John." Without making any attempt to rise, he extended a hand for John to shake. "I'm Franklin Chester, your psychologist."

In sudden alarm, John furtively dove into the booth and blurted in a hoarse whisper, "Did you have to announce you're my shrink in front of everyone?" The good doctor did not answer at once, but just started to guffaw with a rumbling sound like a distant thunderstorm. "No one here even heard me!" he guffawed at last. "Nobody pays any attention to anyone or to anything that is said in the Wilted Chicken. It's better than a stuffy office with a curious receptionist having an ear glued to the door. It's the ultimate in privacy! And you get to eat while working, too!"

John shook his head in disbelief, while staring at the big man's ample belly. It was obvious he met many patients here, but John was still so appalled at the thought that he blurted, "You have GOT to be kidding! This place is about as private as an airport terminal! Are you crazy or something?"

This time the doctor laughed out loud with a sound similar to breaking glass. "Am I crazy?! Is that what you just asked me?" He laughed some more, making his belly bounce around like a bowl full of jelly. Then he bluntly said, "My boy, YOU are the one that is supposed to be crazy, coming to see a shrink!" He giggled some more.

John stared, goggle eyed. "I thought shrinks were never supposed to call their patients crazy!" he blurted. "Isn't that labeling, and harmful to the patient?"

"Probably," said Dr. Chester good naturedly, his eyes crinkling. Then he waived to the food spread across the table. "Help yourself. It's all good stuff--the best the Wilted Chicken has to offer!"

John stared at the greasy fries, partially purple onion rings and half eaten green burger. "No thanks. I ate before I came," he lied.

The good doctor laughed heartily again, then stuffed several fries into his mouth at once. He chewed contentedly away at the rancid things, looking for all the world like a mindless cow chewing her cud.

THIS was supposed to be one of the most renowned shrinks in the city?! John shook his head in disbelief.

"Well, my boy," said Dr. Chester between chews, "I strongly suspect you are wondering right now why I have the reputation of being one of the more sought-after shrinks in the city." John gulped in surprise, while Dr. Chester burped. Then the doctor's brow furrowed, and he started scratching his goatee. "I often wonder that myself. I have no idea how these ridiculous rumors get started. I am, after all, nothing but a second rate shrink more interested in a greasy burger than any heart-wrenching thing a patient might say to me!" Then just to prove it, he took a big bite out of his half eaten burger, which made a rather sickening squelching sound as it went into his mouth.

John just stared, open mouthed. "I wouldn't do that, if I were you," said Dr. Chester unexpectedly.

"Do what?" asked John in confusion.

"Let my mouth hang open. Not with all the flies that live here in the Wilted Chicken, at any rate." John's mouth snapped instantly closed, and he looked around at the buzzing flies that seemed to be everywhere.

"So, tell me about yourself," said the doctor, after picking up an onion ring (dislodging several flies in the process) and starting to twirl it around in a circle on his finger. "Why did you come to see me? Or perhaps more to the point, who put you up to it, eh?" He gave John a knowing wink.

"My grandpa," said John, making the doctor's smile broaden even more. "He's paying for our sessions. I kept telling him I didn't need to see a shrink, but he insisted. He thinks I have unresolved psychological issues that I need to work out."

"And do you?" asked Dr. Chester with another burp. He started twirling his onion ring faster, and it looked like the greasy thing might disintegrate in mid air, and send pieces flying in all directions. John instinctively shrank, hoping none of the greasy pieces would land on him.

"I used to have issues, but I don't anymore," said John firmly. "Not after working for Big Jim and finally coming to myself. Not after escaping from Steve. And especially, not after giving it up for good."

There was silence at their table for a minute, punctuated only by the continuing shouts of the unhappy employees and the endless murmur of the patrons. When John did not offer more, Dr. Chester asked, "Gave WHAT up for good, might I ask? Or is that too personal to tell your shrink in a crowded fast food place full of thugs and outlaws?"

John rolled his eyes in disbelief at the big man's utter lack of tact or even the faintest attempt at the "bedside manner" one would expect of a person trained to deal with people's tender emotions. Suddenly he came to a quick decision. Since grandpa had already sent the doctor a check in the mail for this session, he would go through with it--but TODAY only. Best just to get this nonsense over quickly and leave, making sure never to see this quack again.

"The thing I got over was being gay," announced John bluntly. He watched closely, to see what reaction the doctor would display. Many people tended to react with startled embarrassment when he made this type of announcement. Indeed, he knew that many gays practically live for the gratifying looks of horror they receive and the attention they get upon making such a grand pronouncement. But the doctor was completely unmoved, and continued to chew placidly on his rancid French fries with a circular, cow-like motion to his mouth that reminded John of his mother's clothes dryer when in use.

"Didn't you hear me?" asked John with a sudden flash of anger. "I said I used to be gay, but got over it."

"Sure, I heard you," said Dr. Chester. "That's what I get paid to do, you know--to listen." He stopped chewing for a minute, and started to stroke his goatee again, as if in deep thought. "It's strange, when you think about it. You pay all this money to some stupid shrink

9

who's supposed to help you deal with all your problems, and all the lout does is sit and listen! It makes absolutely no sense!"

John smiled suddenly. "You've got that right," he agreed heartily. "Even if I DID have some remaining unresolved problems--which I don't--I don't see how a shrink like you could help me. Especially if he does nothing but sit and listen while eating rancid food."

In response, Dr. Chester snatched up an onion ring and held it out to John. "Have an onion ring," he said. The greasy thing wobbled in his hand, as if begging John not to put it into his mouth. "There is no problem in all the world that cannot be solved by eating a good onion ring."

John rolled his eyes again. This guy was an absolute fruitcake! HE was the one that needed to see a psychologist! "No thanks," said John abruptly. "Look, you're supposed to be the doctor here, and to tell me what to do so we can get this over and I can go home. So what do you want me to do?" He frowned angrily at Dr. Chester.

The good doctor abruptly stuffed the onion ring into his mouth and then said in an oniony, garbled voice, "I guess that IS what I'm supposed to do, isn't it? Well, why don't you start at the beginning. Start by telling me what led you to believe you were gay." He smiled at John, revealing green onion pieces stuck between several of his teeth.

"Ok," said John, while looking quickly away. To himself in his own mind he added, "Now we're finally getting started. Thank heavens. This place smells worse than a gym locker room!"

Dr. Chester took another squelching bite of his burger. John opened his mouth to start, then suddenly shut it again. And this time, it wasn't because of the flies.

With a sudden jolt, John realized that no one--ever--had asked him this question before. Not his freaked out mother when she'd found out, or any of his sisters. Not his grandpa, who'd just got madder than a wet hornet when he'd first heard of it. Not any of the people that knew him. They had all THOUGHT the question in their own minds to be sure, but no one had ever dared ask him before. All they had done was instantly judge him, which had just as instantly built a wall between them.

So, he had never had to answer this question before. And while he thought he knew the answer, he suddenly found it surprisingly uncomfortable to vocalize it into actual words.

"Well ..." he began at last, fumbling suddenly with one of the onion rings that lay sprawled on his side of the table. "In answer to that question ..." he paused, groping for words. "To begin with ..." he paused again.

Dr. Chester smiled. "My boy, I may be fat, and I may be kind of stupid, and I may be a nut--but one thing I am NOT is a judge. Anything you tell me is still yours, and I won't judge you for it. I won't say anything about whether your choices or actions were good or bad, nor will I talk about what you tell me with anyone else. Like I said before, I get paid the big bucks to just sit and listen--while stuffing my mouth with these delicious Wilted Chicken offerings."

John smiled weakly, then opened his mouth and started talking. And it was suddenly as if a dam had broken, and his story was gushing out, utterly free to be told for the very first time ...

CHAPTER TWO

"I grew up with my mom and two sisters," began John. "I never knew my dad. He bailed on us when I was a baby, and none of us has seen him since. My mom is the firm, no-nonsense kind, and has always been kind of bossy. My sisters are both older than me, and were already into makeup and boys when I was just a toddler. We had a pretty good life, I guess. Nothing too out of the ordinary. I was just a normal kid, growing up in a normal, single parent home ..."

John stopped abruptly, struggling with himself. What came next was something new--or at least, if his mother and sisters ever were to hear it, they would think it was new. His grandpa also didn't know a thing about it. It was, in fact, one of John's darkest secrets, and was something he had kept inside for as long as he could remember.

But for all John's efforts at so closely guarding this secret, he suddenly felt no hesitation in telling it to the big, fat doctor chomping in front of him on unhealthy food. Somehow John just knew there was nothing to worry about. He probably wouldn't see the fat old geezer again, anyway.

Dr. Chester smiled at him, while continuing to chew in his cow-like way. "Go on," he said encouragingly.

"Well ..." began John hesitantly, "it's like this. My mom had a full time job for as long as I can remember. So when I was little she put me in daycare. There were lots of other kids in it too. There was one boy in particular named Kyle who was kind of a big bully. Sometimes he did things to some of us smaller boys behind the tree during recess that the teacher didn't know about, and which none of us could prevent. Nasty things. Things that you're not supposed to do ..." John's voice trailed off. Just how was a person supposed to describe sexual abuse, anyway?

"How long did this go on?" asked Dr. Chester curiously.

"Oh, I don't know," responded John. "Maybe a year or two. When I left the daycare, I never saw Kyle again. I kind of put those memories out of mind. For a long time I didn't think about them. But sometimes I would wake up at night sweating and crying. I never could tell anyone why."

John stuck his finger in the middle of the greasy onion ring on the table in front of him, and began to swing it around on the disgusting tabletop. "I suppose," he continued slowly, "I started thinking I might be gay in junior high. I noticed I didn't seem to be as interested in girls as all the other guys. They'd laugh and talk about girls while we were in gym and other places, and I just didn't get into it like they did. I sort of felt all confused when it came to girls. They were different and somehow unapproachable. I wasn't sure if I was attracted to them or not. They all seemed so distant. Naturally, none of them had any interest in a shrimpy loser kid like me. I just didn't feel comfortable around them, and they definitely didn't feel comfortable around me."

"How was your home life during this time, and while you were growing up?" asked Dr. Chester suddenly. John just shrugged. "A lot of yelling, I guess," he responded. "I didn't have anyone my own age to play with, so I was always trying to get my sisters to like me and pay attention to me. I often mimicked what they did, since I thought that would make them more interested in me. But they would just laugh at me and call me names. As for Mom, it seemed like she was always getting after my sisters about their makeup or the boys they were going with."

John paused a minute, a slight frown on his face. These early childhood memories were not pleasant. "My sisters often talked to each other about their dates and what they did when they were alone with boys on those dates, including some things they weren't supposed to do. They always talked like this out of earshot of my mom of course, but I often listened even though they didn't realize it. I don't remember much more about my home life than that, except mom getting after me a lot for making messes around the house. I was always supposed to be as clean as my sisters."

"Did you have many outside friends?" asked Dr. Chester. "Boys or girls?"

"Not many, and definitely not any girls," replied John. "Like I said, I was kind of scared of them anyway, and they always seemed so distant and unattainable. I was kind of wimpy, and not good at sports or anything. A lot of the other guys made fun of me. I was kind of a loner. I didn't mix too much with anyone. But I did have a few casual friends--other wimpy guys like me. We never went to each other's houses or anything, but we sometimes hung out together at school."

Dr. Chester nodded. "Go on," he said encouragingly.

"Well," continued John, "like I said I started to notice that I seemed to be different than the other boys. I knew girls weren't interested in me, and I still wasn't sure if I was interested in them. I got along better with the wimps and outcast guys that didn't make fun of me. Some of them were kind of weird, but at least they weren't as critical of me. Meanwhile, as I got older I kept having urges and cravings and impulses I didn't understand. I wasn't sure what to do about these feelings, or how to control them." There was silence at the table for a minute, while Dr. Chester continued to munch on his rancid, greasy fries and onion rings.

"Anyway," continued John slowly, "In the summer between 8th and 9th grade, mom decided I needed a more manly influence I guess, so she sent me away for the summer. Actually, it wasn't her idea-- it was my grandpa's. He's my mom's dad. He's a real crusty guy, and always seemed to hate me. I haven't seen him much over the years, since he hardly ever came to our home. But he showed up unexpectedly one day and took one look at me and told my mom he was concerned about how wimpy I was. So they sent me to a camp for boys for 8 weeks."

"We were out in the woods, and there wasn't much to do. The adult leaders didn't pay a lot of attention to us, and spent most of their time playing cards. All except a guy named Michael. He seemed really interested in us, and especially in some of the wimpier boys, like me. He started inviting wimpy boys to spend the night with him in his tent. He said it was so he could tell stories and get to know us better. One of my friends did it, and afterward seemed scared of Michael. He told me not to go if Michael invited me, but he never told me why. Finally Michael asked me and I went and found out why."

"I didn't know what to think after that. I didn't know if it was something I was supposed to have enjoyed, or if it was terrible and disgusting. I thought about it a long time at camp, not sure what to make of it. I just didn't feel much of anything. I guess I was supposed to be upset or angry or hurt, but I just didn't feel anything--anything at all."

"And that's when I started thinking that maybe there WAS something different about me. Maybe I was one of those gay people who can't help it, and who has to accept his gayness for the rest of his life. The more I thought about it, the more I concluded that must be the case. So when Michael asked me to his tent again, I went."

John was silent for a minute, twirling the onion ring around on the table, faster and faster. Suddenly he frowned and blurted, "Now I know that it was all terribly wrong! I only came to realize that when I worked for Big Jim last summer. They never should have let Michael be part of their camp staff! But he was, and he did that to a lot of us, messing us all up pretty bad." John frowned. "It's just like Big Jim says. Sex is not life. It's just a small part of life, and a part you can easily control and can actually live without. But everybody who gets caught up in gayness looks at it differently. For them, sex IS the main thing in life. It's almost all there is to life! Take sex away from a gay, and he has almost nothing left."

"Big Jim?" asked Dr. Chester curiously. "Who's he? Was he at the camp too?"

"No," John said with a slight smile. "I met Big Jim this past summer. He's the one who helped me get over the idea I was gay--to see gayness for what it really is. Until I met him, there was never a man or boy in my life who showed any real interest in me--except for men and boys like Michael, who just wanted my body. Or anyone's body, for that matter."

Suddenly there were a series of shouts and yells from the front of the Wilted Chicken, followed by an ear-shattering bashing and clattering. Looking toward the kitchen entrance, John saw an old man and a young employee involved in what looked like a fight. The old man was waving a pan wildly in the air, while the young employee was trying to use a stack of paper drinking cups as a weapon. He was not doing very well.

"Looks like another employee has decided to leave his job at the Wilted Chicken," said Dr. Chester calmly. "That old geezer is the owner, Mr. Weesl. He always threatens anyone with bodily harm that says they're going to quit. He always uses that same pan, too."

John looked at Dr. Chester with wide eyes. "Shouldn't somebody DO something?" he asked in a tight voice. "If that old guy swings that pan, the kid might get hurt!"

"Not to worry," said Dr. Chester casually, as if bodily injury was completely unimportant. Then to John's amazement he added, "Watch what happens when Mr. Weesl smacks the kid on the head with the pan!" Dr. Chester leaned forward in anticipation of the assault, his eyes shining excitedly. John just stared, appalled. This nutty shrink was actually taking pleasure in some innocent kid getting creamed! Apparently his seeing another human being bashed with a pan was of no real concern. What type of a fruitcake doctor was this guy, anyway?

And then John watched in fascination, as Mr. Weesl hit the kid on the head with the pan-- and it bounced right off again as if the kid's head was made of rubber!

Suddenly all the other employees started to laugh, joined by a few of the older patrons who had seen this nonsense before. The young employee just stared, thunderstruck, unable at first to comprehend what had happened. Then he unexpectedly started to laugh too, while rubbing where his head had been hit.

"The pan is made of rubber," said Dr. Chester matter-of-factly. "It's Mr. Weesl's way of keeping new employees. He drives them till they break, then smacks them with that pan and laughs. Suddenly all the tension is gone, and the new worker realizes it's all just a big game, and no one--not even Mr. Weesl--is taking this stinking place or its food seriously." Dr. Chester smiled, revealing that there were still bits of onions caught between his teeth. "It's a marvelous way to keep new employees, and a wonderful exhibition of caring and good will. That's why I always enjoy coming to this place."

While John continued to stare in amazement at the laughing employees, he saw Mr. Weesl start bashing everyone he could reach on the head with his rubber pan, even some of the patrons. Soon everyone was laughing so hard the place was consumed by general bedlam. Even John found himself laughing, in spite of himself.

Looking back at Dr. Chester, he was surprised to see that the fat doctor had stood up, and was looking at a watch he had produced from an inner pocket. "Well my boy, our time is up for me to sit and listen to your craziness while eating this delicious food." The doctor shook his head sadly. "It was all too short. But of course, it's amazing I get paid to sit and listen at all, while charging exorbitant rates. Meet me next week at this same time, but not this same place." He smiled unexpectedly then added,

"Next week let's meet at the Cheetsya Pizza Parlor on 5th Street! Their pepperoni pizzas are a grease lover's delight!"

Then the fat doctor winked at John, and without another word strode swiftly from the noisy fast food place as if he had not been meeting with anyone at all.

October 11, 2016

Mr. Frederick Anderson
2974 Lerue Lane
San Francisco, CA

Dear Mr. Anderson,

I had my first meeting today with your grandson, John Sanders. I believe the meeting was positive overall. Indeed, John displayed a current distaste for the gayness he once professed, and with which you are so greatly concerned.

I am mindful of your particular concern regarding what brought the gayness idea into

John's head, and whether it is still there. Be advised that when John started telling me his story, he described a number of characteristics common to those who come to believe they are gay. He was raised in a single parent home without a strong, positive male influence, or indeed any male influence that cared about him other than gays. When he became a teen he felt unwanted and undesired by girls his age--who tended to scare him--while boys and at least one man expressed an interest in him. During this crucial time in which he felt sexual promptings for the first time like all teens do, he had blatant, unwanted sexual experiences forced on him. While at first he was naturally repulsed by these experiences--a perfectly normal reaction-- these events joined with other factors in making him begin to wonder about his gender. The idea of possible gayness then grew and grew in his mind, fed by his thoughts. While occasional questions related to gender are normal in the teen years, boys with John's experiential background who overthink the issue often start to conclude they might be gay. Mind you, not every gay person has the same experience, but these are some of the common traits I have seen.

As we discussed when you first retained me to meet with John, gayness is a factor of the mind. There has been no truly conclusive proof produced in any of the numerous scholarly research studies which have been performed about whether gayness is genetic or inherited. None of these tests rise to the necessary level of unquestionable proof or statistical significance to be taken seriously. As I told you before, whether John's father was gay or not--a man who the boy never knew, but who you had a small acquaintance with--is not important. Gayness is psychological, not genetic, and is based on a number of factors. Therapy can alter the patient's thinking on this subject, but whether a person who has labeled themselves as gay continues to think they are that way depends entirely on them. As I stated, it is all in the mind, just as with other psychological issues.

I will keep you posted regarding my visits with John. Attached to this letter is a receipt for the check you sent me in the mail, for John's first visit. I will bill you for my future visits. If you have any questions, please contact me.

Sincerely,

Franklin Chester, PhD

CHAPTER THREE

"My boy," said Dr. Chester while waving a grease-soaked slab of pepperoni pizza in John's face, "you are missing out on one of the great pleasures of life by refusing to eat this pizza!" An ugly glob of greenish cheese gooshed slowly out of the Doctor's pizza slice, and dribbled disgustingly onto the table. "A more delectable pizza has never been invented!"

John's stomach flipped a summersault, then he quickly repeated the lie he had told the good doctor the minute he had arrived at Cheetsya Pizza for his second shrink appointment. "I ate before I came, so I'm not hungry."

Dr. Chester smiled condescendingly, revealing grease stains on his teeth. "Now why on earth would you eat before coming to a restaurant--especially when you knew I was paying for this delicious food?"

John shrugged, trying to think of a convincing excuse. He found none. "I forgot, I guess," he mumbled.

The doctor shook his head once more and took another bite of his pizza slice. As he did so, tiny rivulets of grease smooshed across his mustache and face, and descended in an ugly glob across his goatee.

John turned away from the sickening sight, and found himself wondering for the hundredth time why he had bothered to meet Dr. Chester again. After all, his first meeting at the "Wilted Chicken" had been a complete bust, and he had sworn at the time he would never again subject himself to the old geezer's weirdness. But for some reason, when he'd gotten up that morning, he had suddenly decided to come. He couldn't explain why. He'd even found himself thinking about it all day, off and on, and kind of looking forward to it too.

But now, looking at the good doctor slobbering over his sickening pizza like a mad dog over a rancid bone, John wondered if one his own mental gears had gone haywire. Why on earth had he been looking forward to THIS?

Especially considering the environment the good doctor had plunged him into. Just like the "Wilted Chicken," the fast food joint known as "Cheetsya Pizza" was so noisy from the gabbing of its packed clientele that it was obvious whatever John said would not be overheard by anyone. He and the doctor were alone in the crowd. But the "restaurant" itself was an absolute dive. The roof was sagging, the chairs were all ripped, the floor was so covered with age-old grease from dripping pizza it was impossible to tell its original color, and the place absolutely STANK! It was kind of a lard-mixed-with grease smell that caused John's nose to wrinkle in nonstop disgust.

"Well, let's begin," said the doctor while globs of greasy goo started to drip down slowly from his goatee to the table. "As I recall, you said your grandfather is forcing you to come to these sessions because he dislikes you and thinks you have psychological problems." Dr. Chester smiled pleasantly, and John once again wondered how this nut could have such an awesome reputation as a shrink when he said such blunt, hurtful things.

"And," continued the good doctor, "because you once considered yourself to be gay and lived a gay lifestyle, your grandpa apparently doesn't think you've gotten past it, in spite of everything you've told him. Am I right?"

John simply nodded. "And so," continued the doctor, while nibbling at a corner of his wobbly pizza slice, "at our first meeting you began to tell me your story. But here you have me curious--even though I'm supposed to understand things like this, because I'm a shrink. And this is because your story has some elements that do not seem entirely consistent. You said you were gay, yet when I asked you to explain how you arrived at that conclusion you started by telling me about two sexual encounters you had at a young age --and both times you mostly felt upset! I would not have thought that to be the typical attitude of a gay person."

John nodded again, then smiled slightly. The old coot acted weird, but it looked like his mind was actually in gear after all, in spite of the disgusting food he was eating. "That's pretty much right," agreed John. "I didn't like the first experience in preschool at all, with the bully Kyle. And at first, I wasn't sure I liked the experience with Michael at camp either. But you should also remember how I said last time that I got to thinking about it at camp afterward, and started to think maybe I was gay. After all, I didn't feel as repulsed as I was supposed to by what had happened. And my being gay seemed to add up when I considered my lack of interest in girls, and how I always dealt better with boys. And my second experience with Michael didn't seem repulsive at all. It was like I was a distant observer, watching it all unfold. I was very curious to see if I got upset about it or anything, but I didn't. Like before, I didn't feel much of anything. Most of the time in those days, I felt kind of dead inside anyway."

"After camp, I thought about it a lot. It seems like it was always on my mind. And the older I got, the more convinced I became that I must be gay. Girls still showed no interest in me, and I was uncomfortable around them anyway. A lot of the guys were mean to me, but that's to be expected. I did have a few sort-of friends. They were all a bit nerdy like me, but at least they paid attention to me, and didn't treat me too badly. And when I found out one of them was gay--a guy named Andy--that seemed to reinforce that I was that way too."

"Mmm," murmured Dr. Chester, whether in acknowledgment and agreement with what John had said, or out of pleasure at his disgusting pizza, John could not tell. "The influence of a friend. And then you started to not only think about it, but to talk about it with him, I would guess. And probably you tended to think and talk about it more and more as time went on."

"That's right," said John, looking at Dr. Chester curiously. "How did you know?"

"Just a wild guess," said Dr. Chester while grease bobbled its way across his chin. "Anyway, go on with your story." John found it hard not to watch in fascination as the grease on the doctor's face made a zig-zag track across his whiskers.

"Well," began John, "Andy I soon became good friends. His parents are gay--or rather, his dad is. His dad told Andy from the time he was little that Andy was gay too. Andy's Mom finally just took off and left one day, since I guess she couldn't take his dad's gayness anymore. After that Andy's dad married another man. So Andy has grown up with it for years. His dad had divorced his first man partner before I arrived, and married a second. I started going to Andy's house, and met his dad and his dad's second "'wife." They were very friendly to me, and assured me there was nothing wrong with my conclusion I was gay, and told me that I was welcome there anytime. By the time I was almost

18, I'd been there a lot. And when the bomb dropped, I moved there permanently."

"The bomb dropped?" repeated Dr. Chester with a startled hiccup. "You're too young to have been around when the atomic bomb was dropped on Hiroshima and Nagasaki in 1945!"

"Not that bomb," said John with a smile. "I mean when my mom and sisters found out I was gay. I'd been watching a gay movie one night, and Mom asked about it, and so I told her. She went through the ceiling. Boy, what a lot of yelling and swearing! My sisters joined in plenty too. It was obvious to me that Mom didn't want me in the house and was going to throw me out. So I saved her the trouble and moved to Andy's house. Mom and one of my sisters came to see me only once after that. When they saw Andy's dad and wife, they freaked out. They never came back. In fact, they never even sent me any more Christmas or birthday gifts. It was like I'd died, and wasn't related to them anymore. They just couldn't' accept me the way I was."

Just then, John heard a squishing sound, followed by a yell and a loud thump. Looking over, he was startled to see a large man lying on the floor, moaning softly. Streaked across the floor by his foot was a smashed slice of pizza, with bright, red tomato sauce smeared across the man's shoe.

"Do you need help?" asked John instinctively, rushing over to help the big man to his feet. "Are you hurt?"

"Oh, I guess I'm ok," mumbled the man in a daze as he stood up. Looking down at the smeared pizza slice he had slipped on, he suddenly frowned in anger. "What a lousy, stinking joint this is! I'm going to sue the owner and whoever left that pizza slice on the floor for everything they've got! I could've been killed!" Then without another word he stormed off toward the back of the restaurant, apparently in search of the owner. Meanwhile, a 'Cheetsya Pizza' employee nervously appeared with a mop to clean up the smeared mess on the floor.

Shaking his head, John sat down again at his table. "I think that poor guy's right about how lousy this place is," he said. "They don't even bother to clean up the pizza pieces that fall on the floor! I hope that guy does sue them!"

"If he does, he'll be suing himself," said Dr. Chester, dabbing daintily at his goatee with a napkin, which only succeeded in spreading the grease around even more into his grey goatee hairs.

"Huh?" said John in confusion.

"That was the owner," said DR. Chester with a smile. "He stages his little 'fall' every hour or two, when he thinks his former patrons have all been replaced by new ones. It works wonders at motivating people to clean up their own messy tables before leaving!"

John stared around the restaurant in disbelief. And sure enough, he saw several people who must have seen the fall busily cleaning up their messy tables. This was insane!

"What kind of nut would do such a thing?" asked John. "He's going to knock himself brainless if he keeps it up!"

"Not on that patch of floor," replied Dr. Chester as he took another bite of his greasy pizza. "Take a close look at it ..."

John knelt down and looked closely at the floor. It seemed perfectly normal to him. But he noticed when he put his hand down on it that it squooshed down easily! Pushing on it some more, John saw that this entire part of the floor appeared to have been made of rubber!

Sliding back into his seat in the booth, John said angrily, "Do all the places you eat at have weird rubber things, apparently intended to deceive people?"

"Could be," slobbered Dr. Chester, as he spoke with his mouth full of pizza. "Things are not always what they seem, are they?"

"What do you mean by that?" asked John crossly.

"Take people, for example," said the good doctor as he dabbed at his chin some more with his grease-soaked napkin, making all the grey hairs turn yellow. "Anytime you see someone do something, they always have a reason. The thing they do may make no sense to you at all--in fact, it may not fully make sense to them--but there's still always a reason that they're doing it. And sometimes the reason is not what one would expect, and not the reason they give if they are asked. Often the real reason for their behavior is vastly different from what they say, or even believe. In other words, sometimes the reason is as fake as a rubber pan or a rubber floor. Interestingly, what I have observed is that a fake reason often looks just as real as anything."

"I guess that could be so," said John slowly, straining his brain in an effort to figure out why Dr. Chester was telling him this. "But so what?"

"So, what about the reason for being gay?" asked the Doctor curiously. "Is it fake or real?"

"There's only one answer to that!" said John emphatically. "Big Jim helped me finally see the truth for what it really is, last summer. The whole notion of gayness and being gay is fake! It's all a grand illusion."

"But did you believe that when you lived in Andy's house?" asked Dr. Chester.

"No," replied John. "Not at all. I was convinced then that I was gay. I now know that I wasn't, but I really thought I was at that time. Just like Andy and his dad and wife thought they were. Just like all the gay people I've ever met thought they were. They're so convinced of it, it's more true to them then truth itself. It HAS to be true, because they've built their whole lives on it! Admitting the truth is just too hard for many, I guess. It would be almost like denying themselves, and their very existence. Yet until they face the reality of how fake it all is, they can never escape from it. I suppose that's why many of them are willing to die for it rather than face the truth--as if it's the noblest cause in the world!"

"You mean, they die because of AIDS?" asked Dr. Chester.

John nodded. "Among other things. Andy's dad's second 'wife' committed suicide. They never would tell me how he did it. I just came home one day and found an ambulance parked outside. But as the years passed while I lived at Andy's house, that was something that happened more than once. Gay people would come and go. Some would be married, some weren't. A few committed suicide, and others moved on. Few of the married ones stayed married. They usually got tired of their partner after awhile, and wanted someone knew. That's how Steven came to be there. He was someone new that Andy's dad brought home with him one day."

"Steven," said Dr. Chester curiously. "It seems like you've mentioned that name once before. Was he different for some reason?"

"He was to me," said John quietly. He looked at the doctor for a minute. "He became my husband."

And then without another word, John quickly rose and ran from the restaurant.

October 18, 2016

Mr. Frederick Anderson
2974 Lerue Lane
San Francisco, CA

Dear Mr. Anderson,

My second meeting with your grandson John took place today. Once again I would characterize the meeting as positive. John began today by describing his second experience at camp with a gay man. Much of John's initial conclusion that he must be gay was apparently based on his lack of feeling much of anything from this experience. He described it as unemotionally being outside, looking on. This condition is known as "dissociation," and is a typical self preservation technique used by people in extremely stressful and disturbing situations. Hence, John's conclusion that he must be gay because he "felt nothing" during this experience was in error and was opposite to the truth. Had he understood the true nature of dissociation, he would have recognized that this second experience was as traumatic as the first, and that his dissociation was merely a self preservation technique.

John went on to confirm that his presumed gay condition resulted largely from his excessive thinking about the subject of gayness. As with all thoughts which people dwell on to excess, it started to become real to him. John's gay friend Andy had a slightly different experience, typical of other gays. He was raised by a gay father, who repeatedly told the boy he was gay. It was therefore easier and more natural for him to slide into gayness, concluding that what his father said must be true.

John also told of his mother and sister's reactions when they found out he was gay. In fairness to them, an initial reaction of distaste is understandable, since even the thought of gayness is so contrary to the majority of people that they shrink from it. It takes a great deal of love and concentrated effort to bypass this natural reaction. Unfortunately John's family failed to replace their feelings with patience and sincere caring for John. Loved ones do not have to adopt gayness or accept it as 'true,' and have every right to stand firm in their belief that their son or brother is not gay. But the most effective way to do this is in a spirit of love and patience, avoiding frequent confrontations about the issue. Faced with both love and firm refusal by family members to believe in gayness, many gays ultimately come to change their thinking on the subject.

In John's case however, the reaction of his family merely served to drive John farther toward gayness. He moved to live in a gay house, which only increased the gay emphasis in his life. John briefly described the nature of this gay house which was, sadly, somewhat typical of many such places. I do not wish to trouble you with the details, but I must say your grandson is fortunate that he did not die of AIDS or suicide as do so many in his situation, and as some of the gays in that house did. The gay lifestyle can be a very rather brutal one, in which the participants often switch partners, whether they are married or not. Unless one has lived the lifestyle, it is almost impossible to describe the pain, despair, depression and frequent death experienced by those professing to be gay. In many respects they are the world's ultimate victims, and have a rather unique love/hate relationship with the victim role they have willingly adopted, and which some of them portray as vocally as possible to everyone who will hear them. Most gays carry around with them everywhere they go a strange sense of woundedness. Many of them can neither forsake nor entirely remain quiet about their 'condition.' Indeed, for many gays it is the very act of saying they are gay that brings the attention they both crave and loathe.

I think John and I are making good progress. I will certainly keep you informed of developments as they arise. Our last meeting ended with his mentioning someone named 'Steven,' who seems to trouble him greatly. But he also once again mentioned a mysterious person named "Big Jim" who he said that he met not long ago, who seems to have given him a great deal of help. I hope to hear about both of these individuals in greater detail in our next session.

At my direction, my secretary called John on the telephone and arranged for our third session, since he left our last meeting rather abruptly. We will be meeting at a restaurant known as 'Lettuce Turnip Yer Beets,' which is strictly for vegetarians and health fanatics.

Sincerely,

Franklin Chester, PhD

CHAPTER FOUR

As John rounded the corner of 9th Avenue for his third restaurant/shrink meeting with Dr. Chester, he found himself staring at the last place in the world he would have imagined. He was sure the name "Lettuce Turnip Yer Beets' was a strange name for a greasy restaurant, and had assumed that it would feature greasy meatballs or spaghetti, or some other un-appetizing scumy dish as a specialty, with a sidelight of wilted vegetables. After all, that was the only type of food that nutty Doctor Chester had shown any interest in so far.

Boy was he ever wrong!

The joint was obviously a health restaurant! A massive sign above the door proudly displayed lettuce, cabbage, tomatoes, radishes, and a host of other veggies arranged lovingly in a solid gold salad bowl. The name 'Lettuce Turnip Yer Beets' was written in silver letters above the bowl, while below it were the words, 'The Ultimate in Healthy Eating.' Below this were the additional words, 'Our healthy food will 'turn up' the number of your heartbeats--so you will live longer!'

Why on earth would the good doctor chose THIS place for their next meeting? How was he going to satisfy his craving for grease here?

Shaking his head, John headed for the door. He must have been crazy to agree to a third meeting with this idiot shrink! He had been absolutely positive when he ran out on his last meeting with the doctor that he would never see the crazed lunatic again. But when the shrink's secretary had called wanting to set up another appointment, John had found himself saying 'yes,' to his own surprise. And just as before, he had also found himself oddly thinking about the coming meeting all day, in a bizarre form of dreaded anticipation.

And now he was here. As John pushed open the door, he was startled by the dramatic difference between this eating place and the two where he had met the doctor before. The place was squeaky clean and light and airy, with meticulously polished tables, perfectly arranged chairs, and an atmosphere of contented healthiness conveyed in part by the playing of classical music. Well dressed waiters served the numerous patrons with a smile, and the food looked actually edible. The place was nearly full, and once more was filled with the low murmur of many people talking to each other.

"Welcome, John!" sang out a voice to John's left. Turning around, he saw Dr. Chester sitting at a booth near a window. In front of him were two bowls of crisp, fresh salad, and at the side of each was a tall glass of what looked like lemon juice. "Come and enjoy a healthy repast, sure to extend your life for at least ten years just by looking at it!"

John took a seat and stared at the doctor for a moment. Finally he blurted, "What's going on? I thought you liked greasy food!"

The doctor turned a bit red, and looked distinctly sheepish. "I do--or rather, I did," he answered in an embarrassed tone. "But a few days ago my doctor gave me some disturbing news about my cholesterol level. He even asked if I had a preacher in mind for my last rites! I decided then and there that perhaps I should forego the delights of greasy food. Either that, or I had better quickly take out a plan at a funeral parlor."

John laughed, in spite of himself. Dr. Chester stabbed a forkful of salad and looked at it distastefully. He then put the fork into his mouth and began to chew slowly. The scowling expression on his face clearly showed disapproval, but he forced a smile and said, "It's good!" He grimaced some more, then added in an obvious effort to convince himself, "Very good!"

He sighed suddenly and put the fork down. "It just isn't as pleasant to my taste buds as grease. But at this point, it's either taste and death, or tastelessness and life." He speared another forkful of salad and stuffed it into his mouth. After chewing for a moment he said, "You know, it really isn't bad, in its own crunchy way. I think I could perhaps get used to it. Maybe I could even come to like it."

Suddenly he looked at John and said, "You know, the actual truth is that I owe my life and my new resolve regarding this diet to you."

"Me?" responded John in surprise.

"You," repeated Dr. Chester firmly. "You overcame the idea you were gay, which if believed in and carried out long enough can become a physical addiction. Surely then I should be able to overcome my fondness for and addiction to greasy food."

John laughed. "You're not serious. You're using ME as a positive example?" The thought was utterly ridiculous.

"Certainly," said Dr. Chester. "And why not? You are as much to be admired as anyone, I should think."

Now it was John's turn to blush scarlet. "That's nonsense!" he said defiantly. "No one would want to follow my example. No one could learn anything from my experience."

Dr. Chester just smiled. "You'd be surprised, my boy. But enough chit-chat. You're here so we can deal with your alleged problems, not my real ones. So let us return to your narrative. As I recall, you ended our last meeting by mentioning someone named 'Steven.'"

Instantly John's face changed, and he returned the doctor's curious look with a stony expression. "Yes, that's right," said John in a tight voice. "Steven was one of the gays that moved into Andy's house. And with time he and I got married."

"Interesting," said Dr. Chester in an off-handed way, as if he didn't really care. He took another forkful of salad and grimaced anew.

"What's so interesting about it?" retorted John hotly. "Gay marriage happens now, since it's been legalized."

"True enough," agreed Dr. Chester. Then he added with a curious look in his eye, "Were you in love with Steven?"

"NO!" spat John viciously. Dr. Chester just nodded. Then John ran a shaking hand through his hair. "But I suppose at the time I thought I was. After all, gays always say they're in love with their partner. It's all part of the game they play. Only later from Big John did I learn it's not love at all, just lust. At any rate, I played the game too, and so did Steven. He was the man in our marriage, and I was the woman."

"And was it a good marriage?" asked Dr. Chester.

John swore. "About as good as any gay marriage you'll find. Constant abuse. A never-ending obsession with sexual gratification. More abuse." He ran his hand through his hair again. "If you could have taken the sex out of our so-called marriage, there would have been nothing at all. That's what it was all about. That's what it's always about with gays. There is nothing else. They worship sex. It's their god. And anyone who threatens that worship is a demon and needs to be attacked. And always, constantly backing it up is the unstoppable notion that gayness somehow can't be helped-- that we're helpless pawns, unable to control our urges, and are NOT gay by choice. No gay will ever admit gayness is a choice. That destroys gayness. So he will fight until his dying breath to prove that he has no power over his attractions and gayness--none at all."

"And is that true?" asked Dr. Chester quietly. "Does a gay really have no choice about being gay?"

"Of course he does!" responded John without any hesitation. "It IS a choice, pure and simple, no matter what any of them say. Just like your choice to eat greasy food or salad. The choice gets easier with time, and becomes so automatic you come to think it's always been that way, and there somehow is no choice. But like all choices, it comes with a consequence. The choice of eating greasy food leads to obesity, high cholesterol, and maybe death. The choice of gayness leads to depression, a feeling of worthlessness, sometimes AIDS or suicide, and a never-ending entrapment. As long as you keep following the choice you can never escape it, any more than a fat man can escape his big belly. It's always there--ALWAYS--eating at you, making you feel like scum."

John stopped abruptly in embarrassment, staring down at Dr. Chester's big, fat belly. His face turned scarlet once more.

"My fat belly does tend to always be there, doesn't it?" said Dr. Chester matter-of-factly. Then he gently started to laugh, making the rolls of fat on his belly bounce around once more like a bowl full of jelly.

John smiled, then caught himself and forced himself to look serious. Not knowing what else to do, he picked up his glass of lemon juice and took swig. Instantly his mouth puckered and after he swallowed in surprise he gasped, holding his throat.

"It's unsweetened!" he screeched. "UNSWEETENED LEMON JUICE!"

"I thought you knew," said Dr. Chester, taking a tiny sip from his own glass, and puckering up as well. "They say it's very healthy and good for you."

"If it doesn't kill you first!" cried John.

"Ah, but what is life and death, and things that kill and things that don't?" said Dr. Chester suddenly, extending his arms in a grand gesture. "Things are not always what they seem, and what initially looks desirable often isn't." Then he suddenly stared intently at John. "Is there anything else you want to tell me about Steven?"

"Only that I came to hate him," said John viciously. "I came to hate him with everything in me. He represented all that was ugly and abusive and evil, not only in him but in me. And that's why my hate for him was so great-- because it represented hatred of me, most of all. I let him be what he was to me. And I secretly hated myself for it. It was that type of self-loathing that makes you wish you were dead. And I guess Steven felt the same way about me, because one day he took me up into the hills and abandoned me to die. And I decided that he was right, and that I should die."

Dr. Chester raised an eyebrow in surprise. "Took you out to the hills, like an unwanted puppy you say? How unusual, even for a gay tired of his mate."

John just scoffed. "It's just one of many ways gays cast off their partners. We went up into the Sierra Nevada Mountains, in an extremely remote area. He just pulled over to the side of the road and told me to get out. When I didn't move he shoved me out, then took off in a shower of dust. I never saw him again. I later learned he hanged himself a few months later, after taking another wife in a gay marriage."

"Interesting," said Dr. Chester again, raising his other eyebrow. Suddenly he pointed with his fork at John's bowl of salad. "Come along, lad. Eat up. It's actually quite good, you know." He said this last bit with a mild grimace. "Especially that crunchy red stuff they call radishes, that make your eyes water."

John suddenly let out a breath of air, and smiled. Then without a word he speared some salad with his fork and jabbed it into his mouth. To his surprise, it tasted quite good. "Hey, you know, this isn't bad," he said to Dr. Chester as he speared another forkful. "Tastes almost as good as Rainy's salad, up in the mountains."

"Rainy?" asked Dr. Chester curiously. "That's a name I haven't heard before. Who might that be?"

Before John could answer, an older man in a waiter's outfit approached the table. "Mr. Franklin, sir," he said in a husky voice. "Excuse me, but a telephone call has come in for you." The older man looked critically at the big man's salad bowl. "You don't like it? I thought your usual would be fine for--"

"Telephone, you say?" interrupted Dr. Chester, rising quickly to his feet. "Where's the phone?"

The old man looked startled. "Right where it's always been," he replied in surprise. Dr. Chester grunted, then ambled off toward the far end of the restaurant.

"For cat's sake!," said the old man, "he doesn' like the salad? What's wrong? It's just like always!"

"Excuse me," said John, looking at the man curiously. "But has Dr. Chester eaten here before?"

The waiter threw up his hands. "Has he eaten here before?! Are you a kidding? All the time, the big man comes here. Loves this place he does, or at least so he says!" The old waiter looked accusingly after the doctor. "But maybe he's not telling the truth!" Then he walked off in a huff.

John looked down at Dr. Chester's salad in confusion. This wasn't making sense. The doctor LIKED salad? How could that be? Why would he make a pretense of hating it to John? What kind of game was this?

John looked over to where he could see Dr. Chester talking with someone on the telephone. The doctor saw him and waved. A moment later he hung up and came back over to the table. "Sorry, John, but I've got to go. One of my patients has an emergency. He's locked himself in his car, and won't come out."

"That's an emergency?" replied John.

"It is if you happen to pull your car onto a freeway onramp, then stop," replied the doctor. He looked sharply at John. "I saw you talking to that old dude, who I believe is the owner of this place. No doubt he was saying something about how I eat here all the time and like the food!" Dr. Chester grimaced.

"That's right," said John in surprise. "That's what he said."

"Well, like I said before, things aren't always what they seem. In this place they don't need a rubber pan to keep the employees from quitting, or a rubber floor to motivate the patrons to clean up after themselves. But there are three other veggie restaurants within a two block radius, so any trick a restaurant owner can use to make new customers think their place is popular and that the person treating them to lunch eats there all the time is fair play."

"I see," said John with a slight smile. "So, there's no rubber here. Just lies."

"The only thing that bounces here are the checks of some deadbeat customers," said Dr. Chester. "And as for lies, where can anyone go to escape those? Aren't they all around us?"

John just nodded. And with a quick "good-bye" and the statement that he would have his secretary call John to make the next appointment, Dr. Chester disappeared out the door and was gone.

As John watched the doctor walk quickly toward his car, he found himself wondering two things. First, did the big man like salad or hate it? In other words, who was lying--the restaurant owner, or Dr. Chester?

The second question was more practical. What nonsense restaurant would be the setting for their next ridiculous appointment?

October 25, 2016

Mr. Frederick Anderson
2974 Lerue Lane
San Francisco, CA

Dear Mr. Anderson,

I had my third session with your grandson John earlier today. He indicated that he was at one point involved in a 'gay marriage' with a man named Steven. Interestingly, this Steven character eventually took your grandson out into the mountains and kicked him out of his truck. Probably Steven was just trying to send John a message, but John took it as an attempt to kill him, and then concluded he would indeed kill himself. I suspect his suicide attempt will be the subject of our next session. I might add that Steven committed suicide a few months later.

Do not be too alarmed at the mention of suicide. John currently appears to be stable and not inclined toward any such action. But among gays, suicide is unfortunately rather common. It is hard to put into words the peculiar type of self-loathing that many gays harbor towards themselves, and which John articulated so well in our visit. While many gays live and breathe for attention--rarely caring whether that attention is negative or positive--the dissonance of their lifestyle ultimately catches up with them. It should come as no surprise that suicide is often resorted to as a presumed escape from the difficult issues they face.

Our next appointment has been set by my secretary for next week at 'Lilly's Limpid Liquid Limelunchery.' I would not recommend this establishment to anyone who is not fond of sour, vegetable drinks.

I think the next session will finally reveal the identity of the mysterious 'Big Jim' who John has referred to more than once, as well as an unknown person he recently mentioned named 'Rainy.'

As always, I will keep you posted of developments as they occur. I note that your bill for the last two visits is past due, and a renewed notice of amounts owing is attached to this letter.

Sincerely,

Franklin Chester, PhD

CHAPTER FIVE

The sound of several fruit mixers racing on high met John's ears as he stepped tentatively into 'Lilly's Limpid Liquid Limelunchery.' When Dr. Chester's secretary had called to make this latest appointment, John had requested her to repeat the name three times before he finally got it all down. Why anyone would name their business in such a preposterous way was beyond him.

But as John took a look around Lilly's restaurant, he began to see that perhaps the unusual and nonsensical name was appropriate after all. The entire atmosphere was lit by alternating green and yellow lights, which flashed on and off with annoying irregularity. The tables were shaped like garlic cloves, while the chairs each looked like a zucchini squash with one end lopped off. The music reverberating through the joint sounded like a mix of the beetles and hillbilly twanging. Clearly, Lilly's was no ordinary place to eat.

"Over here, John!" called out big Dr. Chester, waving from where he sat on a zucchini chair on the far corner. On the garlic clove table in front of him rested two large glasses full of an oozing, greenish liquid. John's heart sank as he came up to the table, knowing that one of the drinks was for him. It did not look very appetizing. In fact, it rather looked they had ground up a few hundred green caterpillars in a fruit mixer.

Dr. Chester took a small sip of his greenish goo as John sat down. He smacked his lips contentedly, and said, "Not bad. Has a tangy taste, sort of like mustard mixed with eggnog. But not bad, really. Have a swig!" He smiled at John, revealing that the green goo had stained his teeth.

John's stomach lurched. "No thanks," he said hastily. "I'm not very thirsty."

"Ah, but this is more than a mere thirst quenching beverage," said Dr. Chester. "It is supposed to be extremely healthy and to prolong one's life--as long as you keep drinking these every day."

John blurted, "Maybe so, but if you had to drink these every day, would life be worth living?"

Dr. Chester suddenly extended his arms in another one of his bizarre gestures of grandeur. "And who said life was ever worth living? But you must admit, it sure beats the alternative." Then he gave John a shrewd look. "At least, it beats the alternative for SOME people. As I recall, you were going to tell me what happened after you decided to kill yourself. I'm happy to see you did not succeed."

John smiled faintly. "Right," he said absently. "After Steven let me out, I just stood on the road for a long time. I looked up the mountain and down the mountain, and up the road where Steven had gone, and back along the way we had taken to get there. And suddenly it seemed utterly futile to make any effort to go anywhere. So I just sat down on the road and closed my eyes."

"Hmmm," said Dr. Chester, taking another swig of his greenish goo. "A very effective method to terminate one's life, as long as there is frequent traffic on the road."

"There was no traffic at all up there," replied John. "As I lay there with my eyes closed, it seemed like my whole pointless life paraded across my mind. And as I looked at everything I had done and the life I had lived, I suddenly wanted more than everything in the world to just end it all. And more than anything else, I wanted to end this gayness inside me, so I wouldn't be trapped and victimized by it anymore."

"But in spite of my resolve to kill myself, I suddenly felt so relaxed lying there in the sunshine in the middle of the dirt road that I decided to postpone my death for a little while. It was so peaceful there that I eventually fell asleep. I must have stayed that way for a long time, since it was almost dark when I woke up."

"And that is when you came to your senses and decided life was worth living after all, right?" asked Dr. Chester. He took a big swig from his green drink, which gave him a green mustache over his gray, whiskered one. The green goo started to drip down into his goatee, but the crazy doctor made no effort to wipe it away.

"No, I was still determined to kill myself," said John simply. "Since it was starting to get cold, I thought exposure was the best way to do it. And I decided it would be even colder and lead to even quicker death of I went up the mountain instead of down. So I started stumbling up the mountain. I tripped over boulders and sagebrush and logs, but I kept going. It got dark before long, and very cold too. But I was happy at that. I looked forward to dying. It would finally bring closure to a worthless life."

Dr. Chester merely nodded, as if he was in full agreement that John's life was worthless.

"I must have staggered up that mountain most of the night," said John. I started to get impatient about dying, and wondering why I wasn't dead yet. I was shivering like crazy, but my stubborn body wouldn't die! It was only much later that I realized that because I kept moving uphill, the exertion probably saved me. If I had just had enough sense to sit down and be still, I probably would have croaked like I wanted to."

"And if you had, I wouldn't be listening to you right now, or collecting my whopping, excessively high fee," added Dr. Chester. He smiled sweetly, then took another swig from his green goo. "So thank you, for not thinking to sit down and die."

John just rolled his eyes at this callous statement, which was typical of the silly shrink. Then he continued with his story. "Light was starting to come into the east when I finally got so exhausted that I flopped down on a log. I was breathing hard, and knew the end had to be near. I kept hoping a mountain lion or a bear would come get me, but none did. I lay there for awhile, then suddenly was startled by the sound of someone coming. I jumped up and found myself facing one of the biggest men I had ever seen. He was dressed in thick clothes and was carrying an ax. He looked kind of mad, and for a minute I thought he was going to chop me with that ax."

"And this was Big Jim, I presume," said Dr. Chester with a contented sigh. "We meet him at last."

"It was," agreed John. "He took one look at me and knew I was gay. Of course, I hadn't shaved and was wearing a dress and ear rings, so it wasn't hard to tell. We just looked at each other for a minute, then he said, "Come with me." He turned and started to walk away, but I didn't follow. So he came back, caught me by the scruff of my neck and dragged me after him."

"Sounds like a nice, friendly fellow," commented Dr. Chester casually.

"He told me later he could see I was shivering like crazy and was probably suffering from hypothermia, so he had to get me to a warm place as quick as he could. Anyway, I didn't care. Being dragged or beaten was common in the gay house, so it was nothing new to me."

"After walking and being half dragged for several minutes, we came to a log cabin in a small clearing. Smoke was curling out of the chimney, and there was a light in the window. As we came up to the door, I saw a woman's face peering out at me. She looked frightened. Then we were inside and Big Jim shoved me in front of the fire. I just sat there shivering for a long time, not caring about anything, while Big Jim and Rainy talked low in the background. I could see their little baby boy in a crib, not far to my right, while a mangy collie dog was snoozing on my left."

"Rainy?" said Dr. Chester. "Ah, yes. You mentioned that name in our last session."

"She's Big Jim's wife," said John. Without realizing it, and because he was so caught up with his story, John raised his green glass to his lips and took a sip. The sudden taste in his mouth brought him back to reality, but to his surprise, the mixture tasted quite good. "Hey!" he said with a sudden smile while staring at the glass. "What IS this stuff?"

"Avocado, almond milk, lime and bananas," said Dr. Chester. "With a little brown sugar for sweetening of course," he added.

"Wow!" said John, taking another sip. "How can anything that looks so disgusting and has such weird ingredients taste so good?"

"It is rather pleasant," agreed Dr. Chester, taking another drink which enlarged the green mustache that now completely covered his regular gray one. Green drippings continued to drop down onto his goatee, and from there to the tabletop.

John took another small sip of his green goo, then resumed his story. "After awhile I guess I fell asleep in front of the fire. The next thing I knew, Big Jim was shaking me to wake me up, and telling me it was afternoon and it was time to get to work. I was confused at first, not knowing where I was or who this big guy was who was talking to me. He gave me some jeans and a shirt to put on, and said that normally he'd have me up at dawn to help him with chores, but since I'd apparently been up all night he'd let me sleep through the afternoon just this once."

"Chores, eh?" said Dr. Chester with a chuckle. "Sounds like where I grew up on the farm. We could always use an extra hand, so Big Jim must have been quite pleased."

"I guess so," said John. "But I was not raised on a farm, and didn't know the first thing about chores or what to do. And furthermore, I had no intention of learning. However, big Jim had other ideas!"

"I'm surprised that you agreed to stay and work so willingly," said Dr. Chester.

"I didn't at first," said John. "But Big Jim isn't a guy you say 'no' to very easily. And he said I had to pay him for the food and the jeans and shirt they gave me, by doing some work. My dress was all ripped up and no good, so I had no choice but to take his clothes. Anyway, Big Jim told me that after I'd worked off the price of the food and clothes I could stay or leave if I wanted. That first day I was determined to just get his stupid work done and leave as soon as possible. So I went with him out to a field where he apparently was going to plant some type of crop. There were a bunch of stumps all over the field, from where he'd recently cut down some trees. Our job that day was to dig out one of the biggest stumps in the field."

"Ah, tree stumps," said Dr. Chester with a knowing smile. "I know nothing about getting rid of them. But I would guess the process is not an easy one."

"You got that right!" exclaimed John. "We only worked one hour before dinner that first day, but I was completely exhausted by the time we finished! We dug with shovels all around the stump, and chopped at the roots with axes. Then we got down and tried to push and pull and yank and drag that darn stump out. But it had so many roots underground that it just wouldn't budge. No matter how hard we tried, we just couldn't get the blasted thing out of the ground."

John mopped his brow, as if even thinking about the stump had made him start to sweat again. "Boy, what a job!" he said, absently taking another swig of his greenish goo. "Big Jim is a giant of a man, but with all his strength, he couldn't budge the thing. My puny muscles didn't help much, of course. So we just keep digging around it, deeper and deeper, and chopping out the roots we found with Jim's ax. But it was slow, hard, sweaty work."

A waiter in a bright green outfit came by, and smiling at Dr. Chester said, "Are your drinks satisfactory? Would you like a fresh lime to squeeze into the top of each one?"

"No thank you," said Dr. Chester, while John's stomach flip-flopped at the thought of lime juice being added to his drink. The waiter nodded politely, then disappeared into the crowd.

"So," said Dr. Chester as he scratched his goatee, smearing green goo all over his fingers, "why didn't you leave Big Jim first thing the next morning?"

"That's what I was planning to do," replied John. "Especially when he shook me awake again, when it wasn't even light outside! I'd been so exhausted, I'd slept the night through. But then, without thinking, I found myself stumbling out into the dawn with a shovel in my hand, and for no good reason I can figure out I went right back to work on the same stump. Jim and I worked on it for an hour before coming in to a breakfast of hotcakes and strawberries from Rainy's berry patch. By now little Benjy was up and running around and making noise. That's Jim and Rainy's little boy. And their collie dog 'Risky' was jumping around barking too."

"Hotcakes and strawberries," said Dr. Chester, licking his lips. "That sounds rather pleasant. Is Rainy a good cook?"

"The best!" replied John. "I was so groggy with good food that I forgot to complain about working or to say anything about how I was planning to leave. After breakfast I just stupidly followed Big Jim back out to the stump, and we went at it again. We dug and we chopped and we pushed, and we dug some more and chopped some more, and pushed some more. We fought that stump till our hands were raw and bleeding. We cursed at it and yanked at it, and battled it like it was a demon monster."

"And then suddenly it was lunch time," continued John, while Dr. Chester hiccupped after drinking some green goo too fast, which then caused him to launch into a fit of coughing since he had apparently taken a bit of goo into his lungs.

After the doctor's coughing died down, John continued. "We went inside and had some big beef sandwiches and bowl of stew. And then we went right back out to the stump again. The whole time Big Jim and Rainy hardly said a word to me, and I said hardly anything to them. The only one making any noise was little Benjy and their dog Risky. Benjy kept pretending to be an airplane, and was buzzing around in an annoying way while Risky barked at him."

A distant look had come into John's eyes, and a slight smile played its way across his face. Although he was staring at Dr. Chester, it was obvious that he was not seeing his fat shrink at all, but something else, far away in the mountains. Dr. Chester stared back with big limpid eyes, but his patient took no notice of it.

"There was something about that stump that started to get to me," John said in a low voice. "I knew it was all silly, of course. After all,

I was just a worthless stranger that had happened to show up on Jim's doorstep, instead of dying like I was supposed to. And then suddenly I was working on this stump for no good reason, supposedly to earn my food and clothes. As time went by, and the darn stump kept defying us and laughing at our puny efforts to pull it out, I seemed to become obsessed with it. It's ridiculous, but I seemed to forget everything else. I forgot all about Steven or committing suicide or gayness or how I hated myself or why on earth Big Jim had taken me in, or that it was time for me to go. Indeed, I no longer wondered why Big Jim and Rainy were willing to have me around. I just wanted to get that darn stump out of the ground. Nothing else mattered. That stump seemed impossible to uproot, but I got madder and madder and more and more determined to root the blasted thing out, even if it killed me! And I slaved like a moron all day long on it, too! I worked so hard that my blisters burst, and hurt like sixty! But I didn't care. I worked right through the pain.

After all, I was planning to kill myself anyway, so what did a little blister pain matter?"

"Isn't pain pleasant?" asked Dr. Chester nonsensically. "Some people live for it, you know. At any rate, I presume you got the stump out that day?"

"Not at all!" replied John. "By nightfall the darn thing had started to loosen up a little, but it still wasn't coming out. When we stumbled in for dinner I was so groggy with weariness I couldn't see straight. I hardly had anything to eat, I was so tired. I could barely even swallow. Finally I just slumped at the table and must have fallen asleep, because the next thing I knew Big Jim was shaking me awake again the next morning, where I lay on the little cot they had rigged up for me next to the fire. And then we went out and attacked the stump again!"

"You know, Big Jim should have just hired a backhoe," said Dr. Chester matter-of-factly. "He could have had the stump out in half an hour with a proper use of modern machinery."

John shook his head, while a rueful smile played at his lips. "Not Big Jim. He would NEVER do that. I later learned that he used to be a lawyer in a big city firm, and made lots of money. But he got tired of how false his life in the city was, and how he had to 'play the pretend game' all the time. He had to pretend like his client was innocent--even though he wasn't--and that the person opposing his client was a demon--even though he wasn't. He finally got so sick of it that he took all his money and invested in the mountain property and moved his family there. He was determined to make it into a model farm, and to do it all by hand." John shook his head again. "He was absolutely crazy to even think of doing such a thing. But if he hadn't done it, where would I be?"

"Playing a harp with some angels?" responded Dr. Chester callously.

John chose to ignore Dr. Chester's rudeness. "We finally got the stump out that day. We fought it all day long just like the day before. And right before twilight, with Big Jim pushing with all his might and me yanking away with my puny muscles, and Benjy and Risky running around screaming and barking, and Rainy yelling encouragement--the thing suddenly gave way and came right up out of the ground! It left an ugly, big hole, but it was out!"

"What a relief! I was so happy, I didn't know what to think. And then Big Jim came over to me smiling, and even though he hadn't said more than twenty words to me since we'd met, he said something then that I'll never forget. It was completely out of the blue, and hit me right between the eyes. He just looked at me and said, 'That stump is just like gayness.'"

"Hmmm," murmured Dr. Chester, after draining a healthy swig from his green glass. John could now see that the greenness of the drink itself was somewhat of an illusion. The glass it came in was bright green, enhancing the color of the beverage it contained.

Suddenly a bizarre gonging sound filled the little restaurant. The noise was like a mixture of the chimes made by a grandfather clock and the screeching of a barn owl. Startled, John jumped and looked around in surprise.

"That means it's 4:00 o'clock," said Dr. Chester, pulling out his pocket watch to confirm the time. A dribble of green goo dripped down onto the watch face from his goatee. "Sadly, I'm afraid our session has come to an end." He looked up at John, who for the first time in any of their meetings looked genuinely disappointed that his appointment was over.

Dr. Chester smiled. "I suggest we meet here again next week, at the same time. After all the drinks are good and the atmosphere is sufficiently bland that it does not distract too badly from our task. And perhaps this time I can persuade the talented drink-makers to include a few drops of unhealthy grease in our drinks!"

John's stomach lurched at the suggestion, but he just smiled. He was starting to get used to the doctor's stupid statements. He took another long drink from his glass, then stood up while wiping the goo away from his lips. "Until next week, then?"

Dr. Chester merely nodded.

November 1, 2016

Mr. Frederick Anderson
2974 Lerue Lane
San Francisco, CA

Dear Mr. Anderson,

My fourth session with your grandson John occurred today, and again went quite well. He has finally started to open up in a major way, and to feel more comfortable in talking about the events of his life. I have no doubt this was helped by the fact that our subject of conversation in this session was 'Big Jim,' a large mountain of a man that John fortuitously met in the Sierra Nevada's where his former gay partner Steven dropped him off. For no apparent reason--other than perhaps the advantage of getting some free labor--this Jim character took John under his wing, and put him to work on the farm he was trying to carve out of the wilderness with his bare hands.

Mostly, John described the strenuous effort he and Jim put forth to remove a large and obstinate tree stump from a field that Big Jim was trying to cultivate. It took them three days to do it. In the moment of victory when the ugly, stubborn piece of wood finally came out, Big Jim had the unusual presence of mind to point out how the tremendous task of moving the stump was like the seemingly impossible task of removing the idea of gayness that lodges its deep roots in a person's mind. While John said this Big Jim character was a lawyer before moving to the mountains to become a farmer, I wonder if the big oaf perhaps had a bit of training in psychology as well.

John's narrative today hit upon one of the ways that even firmly believed ideas such as gayness can be challenged and changed. The assumptions on which gayness is based find it hard to survive in the face of brutally hard physical labor, or good, hard work of any kind.

This further supports the reality that such ideas have their origin in the mind, and tend to flourish in large measure because people have too little to do. The farmers and workers of yesteryear had no time to entertain questions about whether they were gay. They were too busy working, and trying to survive.

As always, I will keep you posted of our ongoing progress. Thank you for your recent payment on your bill. While I often wonder if I am truly worth the 'big bucks' people pay me, like most people I am always thrilled when money flows in.

Sincerely,

Franklin Chester, PhD

CHAPTER SIX

"Have a swig of orange-celery-cabbage-pineapple drink!" said Dr. Chester pleasantly as John approached the doctor's garlic clove-shaped table in 'Lilly's Limpid Liquid Limelunchery.' John grimaced at the sight of the yellowish-orange concoction resting on the table before him, and mentally promised himself not to taste even a drop of the sticky-looking mess. Dr. Chester smiled at him sweetly, revealing orange stains on his teeth. There were also orange dribblings on his mustache and goatee, and it was obvious the big doctor liked the disgusting mixture.

"I tried to persuade the owners to pour some grease into our drinks as well, but they just looked at me as if I was mad and told me to go jump in the lake," said Dr. Chester with a happy chirp in his voice. "Since there is no lake nearby for me to jump into, I decided I should add some of the grease myself instead." He pointed to a small cup of grease that the fat man had apparently brought with him.

"I thought your doctor told you not to eat greasy food anymore, or you'd die," said John, his stomach churning at the sight of the grease cup.

"True," nodded Dr. Chester. "And sadly, I must admit that I could not force myself to add this delicious grease to my drink, no matter how hard I tried. I guess my self-preservation instinct is stronger than my passion for the flavor of grease after all!"

John just shook his head and smiled. This shrink was an absolute fruitcake. John had never known anyone so weird.

"And now, if you please," said Dr. Chester, "I am fascinated to learn more about this 'Big Jim' character who took you under his wing in the mountains and somehow helped you discover that you were not gay after all. Just how did he do it? Did he have a magic wand or something?"

"No," said John with a laugh. "He's just a plain, ordinary guy."

"I cannot agree with that," said Dr. Chester. "Not if he was able to accomplish what so many fail to do. So, once again--how did he do it? What did he say or do that made you change your thinking about being gay? You mentioned last time that when you removed the tree stump he immediately identified it as being like gayness. Did you agree with him?"

"Not at first," said John. "In fact, I thought he was nuts to even suggest such a thing. After all, by this time I KNEW I was gay, and couldn't be convinced otherwise. But the thought of being able to root out gayness after tremendous effort did appeal to me. And perhaps it was that hope that made me decide to stay on and continue working with Big Jim to see if I could do it, making me postpone my original plan of going higher into the mountains to kill myself."

"I suppose the mountain lions were disappointed at this sensible decision," said Dr.

Chester nonsensically. "So, carry on. What happened next at Big Jim's cabin?"

"Work!" said John with a laugh. "Nonstop work! Jim and I worked from daybreak till dark every day. After the first and biggest stump was removed, we went on to clear the remaining stumps out of the field one by one. Some of them were almost as hard as that first one, and it took us weeks to get them all out. When the last stump was out, I could hardly believe it. I had never experienced such a feeling of accomplishment! For once in my worthless life I had worked hard and done something I could actually see, and that I could feel proud about."

"After that we plowed and planted the field, then built a rail fence around it with wood we cut down ourselves. We were clearing and planting just like they did in old pioneer days, according to Big Jim. I suppose he was right. I almost felt disappointed when that field was finally done, since that meant I had to face my gayness again, and my decision to leave and kill myself. I suppose a sick part of me had almost hoped the work would go on forever. But I needn't have worried. Big Jim had other plans. He simply picked another nearby spot of ground and we started clearing out the trees and stumps to make another field for planting crops. In other words, we just started all over again. And I was able to forget myself again, and go to work."

"It sounds like a very healthy enterprise, even though I still think a backhoe would have been more logical," said Dr. Chester with a nod. "But are you suggesting that your notions of gayness eventually slipped out of your head from mere prolonged work alone? Surely there was more to it than that!"

"There was," agreed John. "Lots more. As time went on, Jim and I would talk. We talked about lots of things. He was always bringing up his plans for the farm, and the crops he intended to raise, and how he hoped his son Benjy would enjoy a nice, well groomed ranch someday that we were creating. And with time he started to talk about other things too. That's when he told about how he was once a big city lawyer, but hadn't enjoyed having to play the silly game of pretending his client was a saint and the opposite party was Hitler reincarnated. It was all a big game, he said, and was always about money. People sue people almost exclusively over money. They fight over it, squabble and sometimes even kill for it, and then when they die--which can happen at any time--they can't take even a small bit of it with them."

"True," said Dr. Chester with a sigh. "Many have tried to figure out how to do so, but unfortunately no one has succeeded so far. But you haven't told me the most important thing. What about gayness? What did Big Jim say or do to help you change your thinking on that subject?"

"He gave me lots of ideas that made sense," replied John. "It happened gradually while we talked about his life, and I talked about mine. He never passed judgment on my gayness, or belittled me for it. He accepted me the way I was. But he often gently pointed out things that helped me look at everything in a new light, seeing things that I had never seen before."

"For example?" asked Dr. Chester, taking a swig of his drink which left an even thicker orange mustache on top of his grey one.

"Well, there was the logic of it," responded John. "Or rather, the lack of logic of gayness. I remember we got to talking about it one day, and I said I was sure I was born this way, and couldn't help myself. Jim didn't chide me for this, but simply said that what I'd said could not logically be true, no matter how you looked at it. I asked him what he meant by that, and he pointed out that if a person is religious, they'd have to admit that it would be illogical for God to make gay people, then give a commandment against gayness like you find in the Bible. And if you aren't religious and don't believe in God and buy completely into the idea of Darwin's evolutionary theory, then it's just as illogical that beings would evolve into gayness, since that would not preserve the species, which is the main point of evolutionary theory. Those were just two examples he used, but there were others. And his logical conclusion was that gayness could not be hereditary or 'in the genes' as gays claim. It had to originate from something else. And he pointed out that this is why there has never been any statistically significant or adequate scientific proof that gayness is in the genes or is inherited, in spite of all the studies and effort to find such proof."

"Very interesting!" said Dr. Chester, stroking his goatee and smearing orange goo across the whole of it and onto his fingers. Then he moved his finger up to his ear, smearing some orange goo there as well. "Logic! Whoever would have thought of resorting to something so logical?"

"But then Jim went further," said John, forgetting himself and taking a swig from his bizarre orange drink. He was so absorbed in what he was saying that he didn't even notice that he had done so.

"Jim pointed out that if gayness does not originate in the genes or for a physical reason, and since it has to come from somewhere, it must originate in the mind. Our thoughts are very powerful, and shape our entire world. What we believe in becomes our universe. But we will only experience happiness and fulfillment if what we believe is actually true, and is not a false belief. He then said believing you are gay is like believing you own a car which can fly, and is not subject to the laws of gravity. If you act on that false belief, disastrous consequences will follow and you will not be happy."

"On the other hand, believing that you are not gay--and acknowledging that gayness is an illusion and cannot be real--is like believing your car is subject to the laws of gravity. If you act on that belief and drive as if there are laws of gravity, the consequence will be safety. His main point was that you must believe in things that are true in order for them to work for your good and make you happy. You can believe in things that are not true if you want--anyone can--but the consequences will not be good, and you will not be happy."

"Big Jim told me it's like what Jesus said once, 'by their fruits ye shall know them.' Thistle bushes don't produce figs or grapes or fruit you can eat. Likewise, gayness produces bitter fruit such as unhappiness, feelings of worthlessness, abuse and suicide. True principles and true beliefs can be discovered by looking at their fruits and whether those fruits are good or bad. If something makes us feel good about ourselves and other people, if it makes us feel peace and happiness, and makes us want to lift and help others and think positive things, it is true. Things that pull us down are false. But Jim warned that some things give a temporary illusion of happiness and peace, but their real, long-term fruit is bad, so we have to especially watch out for them. The best examples are alcohol or drugs, which give a temporary high. But temporary fruit is not the real fruit. We have to look at the long term consequence, not just short time thrills. And the long-term fruits of gayness are such things as confusion, AIDS, depression, abuse, unhappiness and often suicide."

"Fascinating," said Dr. Chester as he fiddled with his orange ear, spreading the goo even more.

"Jim pointed out that throughout history, many people have tried to believe in things that are not true," continued John. "They have attempted to wish them into being true, or tried to force them to be true, and always with disastrous consequences. For example, there are many ideas besides gayness--in philosophy, religion, politics and other subjects--that people have come to believe over time which are not true, but which some people come to think are true. However, merely believing them to be true does not make them so. We only THINK they are. In a way these ideas become true to us for a time, but they are not really true. And the consequences of acting on those ideas as if they were true are always bad."

"And I suppose, when you heard all this, you readily agreed with him?" asked Dr. Chester.

"Not at all!" said John firmly. "I'd been 'gay' for so long, there was no way I was going to budge from it that easily. In fact, I've hardly known any gays who are willing to admit that their beliefs about gayness may be incorrect. They'll fight any such suggestion, like wildcats. It's not easy to overcome such deeply ingrained thinking."

"So, how did Big Jim overcome it with you?" asked Dr. Chester once again.

"A lot of what he said was based on logic," said John. "But a lot of it went beyond logic, and simply rang true inside regardless of whether it was logical in my head. As I thought more and more about it, what he said not only started to feel right but it also made a lot of sense. Because my previous ideas were questioned and challenged by Jim in a non-confrontational way, I had to deal with what he was saying. He never called me names or made me feel bad when our ideas on gayness clashed. But he never backed down either, and didn't hesitate to offer his thoughts. At first I'd get angry at his calmness about it all. But I soon learned that it wasn't enough for me to just yell 'you're wrong,' because he would just calmly reply 'why?' In fact, one thing he repeated over and over was that every person who has come to believe they are gay has a duty and an obligation to find out WHY they developed that belief. They do this, he said, by a process of prayer and deep introspection. For some, professional counseling may also be required."

"Prayer and introspection?" said Dr. Chester in surprise. "Really?"

"Yes," said John. "Naturally I resisted this, since I did not believe in God when I first met Jim, just like many gays don't believe in God. But Jim just pointed out that my nonbelief in God did not make God nonexistent, and that the consequence of not believing in God was just hurting me, not God. He pointed out that if I wanted to know if God was real, all I had to do was ask him and he would tell me. But he cautioned me that since God is not me and is a different, individual being who has the right to his own thoughts and methods of doing things, that I had to let God reveal himself to me in his own way and time, and not according to some method of revealing that I came up with in my own head. He told me that if I patiently sought after God, he would reveal his reality to me, and then he would help me understand what led me to believe I was gay. He said it is a lot easier to deal with gayness with God's help than without it."

"And did you follow these suggestions?" asked Dr. Chester curiously. "Did you ask God if he was there?"

"Yes," said John quietly, as he settled back in his chair with a faraway look in his eyes. "Yes, I did." He paused for a moment, as the gentle murmur of the other patrons in 'Lilly's Limpid Liquid Limelunchery eddied around them. Then he said slowly, "I asked him more than once. I started asking every night. I started praying. I slowly developed a desire to really know--to know for sure. God didn't answer me right away. I think he knew that I needed to really want the answer and to struggle for it, in order for the answer to have meaning to me when it finally came. And one morning as I was watching the sunrise over the mountains the answer came. It really came ..."

"Fascinating," said Dr. Chester as he took another swig of his orange goo. "Did God speak to you? Did you hear a voice?"

John smiled faintly. "In a way, yes. It wasn't an audible voice, but it was God's voice just the same. I felt something in my heart that was so real, and so tangible, that I knew--I ABSOLUTELY KNEW--that a separate and distinct being was speaking to me. It was like his spirit touched mine in a unique method of communication I had never known existed. It was a sixth sense of spirit talking to spirit which was absolutely separate from my normal senses. But this communication was so much more powerful! It was more real than if I had seen God with my eyes. I knew he was real at that point. And even better than that, I knew that he loved me and cared for me. And I knew he would help me discover the truth about gayness."

"And did he?" asked Dr. Chester with a mild burp. He rubbed his ear, spreading the orange blotch in his hair.

"Yes, gradually he did," replied John. "I still had a lot of questions and doubts and confusion. I talked about them with Big Jim all the time now, and it seemed like half the time he was always asking me 'why?' Why did I believe a certain way, what was my reasoning, and was this reasoning really reasonable? And when I dealt with these 'why' questions Jim was always raising, it often seemed like God stepped in to help enlighten my mind about the truth of things. And slowly my ideas about gayness started to change."

"It took time though, for me to deal with some of my doubts," said John with a rueful smile. "I had all kinds of questions that had to be answered. Take animals, for example. I pointed out to Big Jim one of the arguments lots of gays use, that gay acts can be observed in some animals, and therefore such behavior must be normal or natural. He simply asked if I also believed it was appropriate for humans to murder and eat their newborns, like polar bears or hamsters do in nature. Indeed, if we rely on animal behavior as our guide, rampant societal murder would be the norm, since carnivores kill for a living. Theft of food by animals is also the norm in the animal world, so laws against theft should be meaningless. Moreover gay animal acts are the exception, not the norm."

"When I tried to dodge this by shifting from animals and saying that I had 'same sex attraction,' he simply asked what caused this attraction--once again bringing up my duty to find the reason by prayer and introspection. I said I didn't know how the same sex attraction came, but he said this was not good enough--there had to be a reason. Since we had already established such an attraction was not from god or nature or my genes, it had to come from somewhere else. When I couldn't give any ideas about where it had come from, he introduced the idea of self-punishments, hidden motivations and frustrated desires to me. And as I prayed about these ideas, I came to better understand how I had developed the false idea that I was gay. In short, God helped me understand the illusion of gayness."

"Self punishments?" asked Dr. Chester curiously. "Hidden motivations and frustrated desires? Although I think I have some idea what Jim might have been referring to, it is fascinating that some lawyer-turned mountain farmer would have come up with such ideas."

John smiled. "Jim's a deep thinker," he said. "He's always thinking, and always trying to figure things out. For example, he pointed out that there are all types of people in the world. Some of them are greedy and insensitive, and really don't care if they hurt others. But other people are more sensitive, and feel guilty or unhappy if they realize they have done something wrong, or hurt someone, or that their life has not measured up. People like this often 'punish' themselves for their mistakes. And if their mistakes are big ones--or at least if they THINK their mistakes are big ones and therefore their punishment should be greater--they resort to harsher punishment. All of these punishments originate in the mind. And the punishment always has to be something detestable or highly undesirable to that person, or it couldn't justify itself as a true punishment!"

"And he therefore suggested that gayness is a punishment, eh?" asked Dr. Chester, raising an eyebrow.

"Yes, in a way," said John. "For many people, that's part of what it is. But he said that humans are complex beings, and not every gay is someone who is punishing himself. Others have other motivations, although what is most common is to have a mixture of many different motivations. Many of these motives relate to psychological stress the person has experienced, often when they were just a child and were vulnerable and helpless. A child who feels rejection from a parent, and even teenagers or adults who feel rejection from others, often feel worthless and will frequently develop health problems, and sometimes very serious ones. And for some, rather than developing physical health problems, they might develop psychological ones, such as an obsession with stealing, or drinking or gayness."

"Fascinating," said Dr. Chester again. "This Big Jim sounds like quite a character.

"He definitely is," agreed John. "He also pointed out the frustration element that drives some to gayness. He said sexual desire with the opposite gender is a natural thing, but if a person does not have a spouse and thinks that the opposite sex all reject him, rather than work to change himself or just exercise self control and go on with life without sex he may turn to other sources for this satisfaction. Some fill their desires with pornography or self abuse, and others with gayness. But the most logical thing for them to do is to overcome their wrong ideas about the opposite sex and come to see that they can find a willing spouse if they work at it."

"He also said that even some married men turn to gayness if their desire exceeds their self control, and if they don't believe they're getting enough satisfaction from their wife. They simply need to learn self control--to be in charge of their urges, and not the other way around. If a person lets their urges control their behavior, they will always be in turmoil. Indeed, he pointed out that many people have lived happy and satisfying lives without fulfilling their sexual urges at all, and that it is not nearly as hard to do this as society tells us. All it takes is for a person to exercise self control and use his or her energy for good causes. In short, you can live without sex and still be very happy and fulfilled. And you will ALWAYS be happier doing so than if you abuse sex, by gayness or pornography or infidelity. Only those who have sex after committing in marriage to the opposite gender experience the fulfillment of it. Those experiencing it in any other way only have a cheap thrill, and are left feeling empty and hollow."

"Most of all however, through a process of prayer and introspection and Big Jim's ideas, I came to see that gayness is created in the mind. Our minds are very powerful. We only do things we have thought in our minds first, and if we don't think it first it never happens, and in fact never even could happen. So whatever actions we take are always preceded by thought. With God's help, we have the power to move our thoughts in whatever direction we want. We don't have to dwell on negative thoughts that might hurt us, or accept false thoughts that lead us in the wrong direction. We can change them to positive thoughts which will lift ourselves and other people. Whatever we dwell on in our thoughts--good or bad, wrong or true--becomes our reality."

"Jim said a lot of the confusion that leads to gayness comes from people having the wrong thoughts in their minds about gender, and gender roles. People often think that men have to be tough and callous, and be into sports or hunting or cars, while women are timid and gentle, care about clothes and have a better perception of feelings. If either gender finds themselves not fitting these molds or that their interests don't fit these gender ideas, they might start to question their gender identity. But Jim pointed out that this is nonsense. There is nothing wrong with a masculine man being gentle or feeling deeply about others, and not getting into 'macho' things. In fact, he said that Jesus proved that better than anyone! He was strong and masculine and independent, but was not afraid to let his deep feelings show." John paused for a moment, staring into space as if seeing something that was not there. "I saw this in Jim, himself. He was very tender towards Rainey and Benjy, and towards all of his farm animals. He didn't speak harshly to them or pretend to be a tough guy. But I came to see that he was a true 'man's man' who felt very comfortable with the way he was. During the time I lived with him, I saw this more and more."

"Most impressive," said Dr. Chester with a hiccup. Suddenly his eyes widened. "But speaking of time," he said while pulling out his pocket watch, "I'm afraid our meeting has run its full course today." He looked across at John. "Would you be willing to come to my office for your visit next week?"

"Your office?" blurted John in surprise. He had become so used to seeing Dr. Chester at bizarre restaurants that he had forgotten the silly shrink had a real office with a real couch-- an office John had never seen or been to. "Sure, I guess. But how come? Are you tired of eating while we talk?"

"ME?" responded Dr. Chester emphatically. "Tired of eating?! NEVER!" Then he added in a sheepish tone. "However, my doctor has encouraged me to fast one day a week to help with my ... shall we say 'weight problem.' I haven't fasted in years, but am guessing it will be easier to go without my precious food if I am away from restaurants, and while I'm busy doing something rather than just sitting at home staring at my refrigerator. And of course the only thing I ever really DO is listen to my crazy patients."

John laughed. "You're not supposed to call your patients crazy, remember?"

"I suppose not," said Dr. Chester with a sad sigh. "But they all seem to enjoy it when I do. I think it makes them feel justified in paying my exorbitant fees." He suddenly pulled out a card and handed it to John. "Here's my office address. Meet me next Wednesday at 2:00." He stood up to go, then added as an afterthought, "And just in case I can't maintain my fast, I'll be sure to order in a Cheetsya Pizza, or maybe one of these delicious orange drinks which I can see you have obviously greatly enjoyed, since you've drunk most of it!"

"I have not!" countered John. Then he looked down at his glass and was shocked to see that the Doctor was right. Almost all of the cup was gone! John had drunk it without thinking, while he had been talking about Big Jim! And he still couldn't say what it tasted like!

November 8, 2016

Mr. Frederick Anderson
2974 Lerue Lane
San Francisco, CA
Dear Mr. Anderson,

I had my fifth session today with your grandson John. On this occasion he spoke a great deal about his mountain friend 'Big Jim,' and the ideas Jim has presented which have slowly changed his thinking about gayness. I must say this Big Jim character has a number of interesting and compelling ideas. He resorted to a combination of logic and common sense in countering the excuses and justifications for gayness that are so frequently thrown around today, such as the justifications of animal behavior or the notion of 'same sex attraction.'

But Big Jim went further. Rather than merely refuting gay reasoning (which is all that most gay critics do) he offered reasoning of his own that tends to explain why some people turn to gayness. He correctly concluded that there is no single reason that applies equally across the board. Rather, some turn to gayness out of frustration, others due to rejection, and yet others from what Jim termed as 'self punishments.' Sometimes these reasons can be mixed together in interesting combinations. Jim also described the gender confusion that sometimes comes when people think they don't fit stereotypes about gender which are portrayed in the media, or which appear to be generally accepted in society. Although not necessarily covering all of the possible psychological reasons for gayness, Jim's ideas are very compelling.

Perhaps Jim's greatest contribution to your grandson's thinking was to inspire him to develop a belief in God. He urged John to pray and to discover for himself if God was real, telling him that if he did this God would reveal himself in his own time and way and would help him discover the truth about gayness.

Commendably, your grandson had the persistence and the desire to make the effort, and as he described it to me, discovered for himself the reality of God. Just as important, he discovered that God is a loving being who wants to help him, and in particular wanted to assist in his discovering the truth about gayness. Armed with this new belief and assurance, John began searching in earnest for the reasons for his own gayness. As he described it, with the help of God and Big Jim, he began to discover those reasons, and came to see his gayness as an illusion.

I sense in your grandson a deep respect and trust for Big Jim. It appears that Jim is the first true 'man' your grandson has encountered that ever showed an interest in him--not a physical gay interest of course, but a sincere caring and concern that has nothing to do with the body. While John has not said so, I believe that one of the ways that Jim has helped him most in overcoming gayness is not so much what he has said, but what he has done. John saw in Jim a gentle but profoundly strong man with a simple faith in God, who was comfortable with himself and his place in the world. This man loved his wife and child, and showed sincere, unpretended interest in others, and particularly in John. John's respect and admiration for Jim created a subconscious desire to emulate him. In short, John observed true masculinity in Jim and saw what life could be like for such a man, and that it could indeed be very pleasant and even wonderful without gayness.

Our next visit will be in my office. This visit may be our last. Your desire from the beginning was to discover whether John is still gay, in spite of what he professes. From our visits so far I believe he is sincere in his declaration that he has put gayness behind him, and indeed now feels that his gayness was just an illusion from the beginning. For whatever it is worth, I intend to tell him that in my professional opinion he is not gay. My doing so is likely to carry greater weight in a professional setting rather than the free-wheeling restaurants we have used for our meeting places so far. These locations created a lighter atmosphere that was helpful in drawing out John's thoughts on this very serious subject, but I think we have mostly passed beyond this need. However, I may bring some food into the office to soften the stuffy atmosphere somewhat.

I am attaching a new bill to this letter. I appreciate your payments, since like all people I like money. I realize that in our society we are not supposed to say that, but in my profession I try to be more bluntly truthful than perhaps I should be.

Sincerely,

Franklin Chester, PhD

CHAPTER SEVEN

"Come in, come in!" sang out Dr. Chester when John poked his head through the office door. "Both the noodles and I are ready for our session today!"

"Noodles?" said John in surprise as he stepped into the shrink's office. As he looked around the room he was surprised to see two bowls of steaming noodles on the doctor's large oak desk. The doctor was resting his considerable bulk on the couch which was undoubtedly intended for his 'crazy' patients, as he called them. There were expensive furnishings and art objects scattered around the room, and it was obvious the good doctor liked nice things.

"But I thought you were fasting," said John as he walked over to the desk to look at the noodles. He was startled to see a pair of chicken feet sticking out of each bowl! His stomach lurched at the sight, and he turned to gawk at the doctor.

"Yes, I'm supposed to be fasting," said the doctor as he jumped up from the couch and came over to the noodles while licking his lips. "But on my way here today I happened to pass this little Brazilian/Asian restaurant, and I found myself going in to see what they had to offer. And on their menu was this delicious concoction of banana noodles and chicken feet you see before you! Chicken feet are considered a delicacy by some in Brazil, perhaps since that's all many of the people can afford."

"You have GOT to be kidding," said John, taking a step back from the desk. "Banana noodles? With chicken feet?"

"Yes," said Dr. Chester, licking his lips again. "Sounds delicious, doesn't it? Have a bowl!" The doctor grabbed a fork and one of the steaming bowls from off the desk and then went back over to the couch. He started munching away at the concoction as if it was the best mess in the whole world.

"I think I'm good," said John simply, not even touching his bowl. He looked around the office for a place to sit, since the Doctor had taken the couch which was no doubt meant for him. But the only other available seat was the doctor's leather chair behind his desk. John tentatively sat down in the soft chair. The doctor took no notice of it.

"Delicious!" said Doctor Chester in a garbled voice as he scarfed down a mouthful of noodles. "You simply must try some."

"Uh, I'm not really hungry," John lied as he watched in distaste while the doctor ate.

"These chicken feet are something else!" said the doctor as he nibbled at one. "Not much meat on them. None at all, in fact. But very tasty in their own, crunchy way."

John shuddered, then swiveled around on the doctor's office chair to look out of the window. He could see the parking lot and Janice's car not far away. She saw him and waved. He waved back. She had said she might go to the nearby mall during his session, but she had apparently decided instead to wait for him right there.

"Smart idea," said the Doctor unexpectedly. John looked over at him, having no clue what the crazy shrink was talking about. He saw the doctor waving one arm wildly in the air, while still holding a chicken foot in the other hand. "These delicious noodles and chicken feet create such a tantalizing aroma they draw lots of flies. Got to keep them away!" John looked around curiously. There were no flies at all in the doctor's immaculate office.

"Now, on to the business of the day," said the Doctor with a happy burp. "We're here to continue our discussion of what made you change your idea that you were gay. And if I remember correctly last time you talked about a number of ideas that Big Jim told you in the mountains on the subject. We also talked about how you came to develop a belief in God, and how God helped you discover the truth about gayness."

"That's right," said John, shuddering again at the sight of the bony chicken foot in the doctor's hand. Perhaps talking about Big Jim would help get his mind off the doctor and his nonsense food. "A lot of what Jim told me combined with the things God helped me to discover as I prayed and thought on the subject. With time I came to see that gayness was just a creation of my mind. And I also saw that if my mind created gayness, my mind could un-create it as well. But in order for my mind to do this, it was essential for me to come to understand and recognize and deal with the underlying causes, such as self punishments, frustration and mistaken ideas, and gender confusion."

"And is that what happened to you?" asked Dr. Chester. "Did you discover and deal with those underlying causes?"

"I suppose I did," said John with a slight smile. "I came to see how I had developed feelings of rejection and frustration and gender confusion which led to self punishments in my life, all of which had led me to believe I was gay. And then I had to deal with them. The mere act of recognizing these things helped a lot in resolving them. But I had to do more. And I found what helped most in dealing with these issues was what Jim calls the 'ultimate weapon.'"

"The ultimate weapon?" said Dr. Chester, looking up in surprise. "Was Big Jim into weapons development as well? Has he developed working laser technology? Or did he create his own atomic bomb?"

"Of course not," said John with a laugh. "The weapon Jim showed me was much different than that, but it is very powerful. I never thought of it as a weapon before I met him. But he helped me see it for the weapon it really is, and with the help of God as I used this weapon I came to see that Jim was right. It's the weapon of forgiveness."

"Forgiveness!?" exclaimed the doctor. "A weapon? Really?"

"Absolutely!" said John firmly. "Most people, gay or not, stay in whatever rut they're in until they can forgive their way out of it. They have to forgive others for the rejection and the hurt they've caused them; accept personal responsibility for their choices and then forgive themselves for having gotten into the rut; and even forgive God if they somehow think he wrongfully allowed them to be swallowed up by the rut in the first place. And in the process of forgiving, they are lifted away from the things holding them back. Until people forgive and accept personal responsibility for their choices, Big Jim said they usually stay right where they are and don't progress in life. And as I began to practice forgiveness, with God's help things began to change for me."

"Fascinating," said Dr. Chester as he propped the chicken foot he was holding behind his ear and took a forkful of noodles. John shuddered again to see the grotesque foot poking out from the doctor's ear as if it had grown there."We psychologists are familiar with the power of forgiveness, of course. But I have never heard it described as a weapon before. What made your friend Jim identify it as such?"

"Because he said it destroys the things holding a person back," said John simply. "When he was a practicing lawyer he saw lots of clients who needed to apply forgiveness a lot more than they needed to win their lawsuit and get the money they were after. He saw that forgiveness would solve their problems far better than anything else possibly could. And he said that if we turn to God to help us forgive, God will do it. He will give us the extra strength to forgive when we don't think we are strong enough to do it on our own."

"Probably more than any other group of people in the world, gays need to forgive,"

127

continued John. "They need to forgive family members for rejecting them. They need to forgive the many people who have exercised their lust on them as they have lived the gay lifestyle. They need to forgive nongays who have judged them as being worthless due to their gayness, rather than exercising nonjudgmental caring and trying to help them. They have to forgive life itself for steering them in the gay direction. Most of all, they need to forgive themselves for having developed and wrongly accepted ideas of gayness, and for concluding they were gay when they were not, because there really is no such thing as gayness. Until they can see the illusion and falseness of gayness and forgive themselves for having adopted it, they can never get out of their rut. They'll stay there forever."

"Forgiveness helps overcome the self punishments and frustrations and other causes that combine in a person's mind, making them conclude they are gay," added John. "When you truly forgive yourself and stop seeing yourself as a failure or as worthless, your need for self punishments drop away. You also gain hope from forgiveness, which will help you deal with frustration, and help in finding fulfilling and positive things to do in life. After all, it's almost impossible for frustration to develop in a person if they're so busy doing worthwhile things and serving and helping people that they don't have time to worry about themselves."

"Fascinating," said Dr. Chester again, as he took another nibble of his chicken foot. "So at the end of the day, forgiveness is a weapon because it wins freedom for you, and helps overcome misplaced thinking?"

"That's right," agreed John. "Jim said most people don't really understand forgiveness, or how powerful it can be. He said forgiveness is really a selfish thing, in a way, because we do it to free ourselves from the millstones around our necks. When we forgive someone, we do it for US, not for THEM. They may not even know we've forgiven them, but we will know. And it will make all the difference for us, even though it may do nothing for them. That's why we need to forgive people whether they deserve it or not. Their deserving it has nothing to do with the need to forgive, or what forgiveness can do for us."

"Very profound," said Dr. Chester with a nod of his head. "I'm curious about something. Did your friend Jim tell you how you can know if you've forgiven someone? Is one quickie 'I forgive you' enough to do the job?"

"Not usually," said John with a smile. "He said you usually have to forgive over and over and over, especially where you've been hurt deeply. In my case, I had to forgive Kyle and Michael and Andy and Steven and my dad and mom and sisters, and especially myself over and over and over again. It took a lot of prayer, and time. Sometimes I was forgiving 50 to 100 times a day--every time I thought about them, in fact! But God helped me do it. In fact, without his help, it would have been so much harder. And I knew I had truly forgiven when I could think about these people without feeling angry or resentful against them."

"Mmm ..." mumbled Dr. Chester while chewing his noodles in his cow-like way. "You mentioned more than once," he said slowly, "the need for a person to forgive themselves. Is that really necessary?"

"Absolutely!" said John firmly. "By far, the most important person we need to forgive is ourselves. And that's also the hardest kind of forgiveness, too. We know our own weaknesses and stupidity better than anyone else, and it's very easy to be hard and unforgiving of ourselves. But Jim said we simply can't rise to the higher levels of peace and happiness waiting for us until we forgive ourselves and see ourselves as inherently good, capable people. God can help us do this if we let him, since he knows all our good points and our bad points, but loves us anyway. I had to forgive myself for concluding I was gay, and for hurting myself and others so badly. It was the hardest thing I have ever done. Even today I have to keep forgiving myself almost constantly, and to avoid the temptation to bash myself for my past dumb decisions. But I feel much better about my life now. I know I have much to offer, and that I'm not gay and don't need to be. And that knowledge mostly came from God and the power of forgiveness."

Dr. Chester nodded sagely. "Your friend Jim missed his calling," the doctor said flatly. "He shouldn't have become either a lawyer or a farmer--he should have become a psychologist!" Then he looked shrewdly at John. "But was forgiveness the only 'weapon' Big Jim taught you to use? Or were there others?"

"Forgiveness is one of the most important ones," replied John. "But there are others. Another weapon or tool for fighting off self-destructive notions like gayness is love. Not sexual or physical love like people think, but real love like God has for all of us. What we need to develop is pure and simple concern and caring for everyone. When we learn how to think more of others than ourselves, and to truly care for them and feel for them and want to help them, we will find ourselves lifted higher into happiness than we ever thought we could go. After all, that's the way God loves. And I came to see this in Big Jim too."

"True love leads to service. You can't have one without the other. Big Jim both loved and served everyone around him. I saw it in the way he would treat his wife Rainy and their son Benjy, and even me. He was always doing stuff for us secretly, trying to make us happy. And while it made us happy to see how much he loved us, it seemed to make Jim the happiest of all. Somehow when he was forgetting himself and giving of himself and serving others, he found himself. I know that doesn't make much sense. But I could see it in his life. It truly was amazing. And it made me want to learn that kind of love, and to serve others as well."

"Ah, the joys of pure love and service," said Dr. Chester with a slight smile. "Love is so wonderfully powerful, yet is so rarely discovered by most people in the world. But those who DO discover this great secret are always the happiest of people. They never wish to turn back to their former, selfish lives."

John nodded. Turning, he looked across the parking lot. Janice was still in the car, waiting for him. She looked like she was reading a book. Perhaps it was the Bible that she always carried with her. She must have felt his probing eyes since she suddenly looked up. Then she waved again. John waved back.

"Are you getting a lot of flies over there?" asked Dr. Chester, rising from the couch and coming over to look around the window. "I wonder if they're getting in through the screen?"

"It's not flies," said John. Then he added softly, "I was just waving to my girlfriend Janice."

"Really?" said Dr. Chester, giving John a penetrating look. "I suppose that's one of the questions I should have asked you--seeing as how you've said you are no longer gay. Just how do you feel about girls?"

John turned a bit red. "They're nice, I suppose. Especially Janice."

Dr. Chester looked out at the parking lot. He saw a young girl looking at him from the passenger seat of a Mazda. He suddenly pulled the chicken foot from behind his ear and waved it at her. She looked a bit puzzled, but waved back.

"That's Janice," said John proudly. "I'll have to explain about your chicken foot later. But after what I've told her about Cheetsya Pizza and the other places we've met, I'm not sure she'll be surprised."

Dr. Chester looked suddenly down at the chicken foot in his hand as if he had just discovered for the first time it was there. Then he put it to his mouth and took a nibble. "Very tasty, in a bland, tasteless sort of way," he said nonsensically. After that he ambled over and plopped back down on the couch.

"So, you now think girls are hot stuff, eh?" said Dr. Chester. "Do they 'turn you on' like gay men used to?"

John shook his head. "No," he said simply. "I never knew what being 'turned on' felt like until I met Janice. It's so much better with her! The whole attraction thing with gay men was just pure, bitter and selfish lust. It wasn't fulfilling at all, and wasn't even real. But just being with her is wonderful. She makes me feel like I'm alive for the first time. I sometimes have to watch my thoughts when I'm with her too, so my actions won't get carried away."

"Oh, really?'" asked Dr. Chester curiously. "And just how do you 'watch your thoughts?'"

John shrugged. "I just do what Big Jim told me. When he was tempted with lustful thoughts he just would tell himself 'my mind is not a trash bin. Trashy thoughts are now going where they belong.' And then he would throw out the trash and immediately get his mind busy thinking about something else that was good and pleasant. Things like his farm, or his son Benjy, or even what he was going to have for dinner. He often said thoughts are like a river. They flow through the course of least resistance. So you have to make an attractive path for them to go--and then they will go there as sure as you're born."

"Besides," added John with a chuckle. "Even if I did try to get physically involved with Janice, she wouldn't let me. She's very level headed and firm minded about things like that. She says you kill love by expressing it too early. It blossoms best when you hold back until after commitments are made and fulfilled--like the commitment of marriage. She has ideas a lot like those of Big Jim."

"Mmmm," said Dr. Chester, nibbling on his chicken foot. "Very profound. I should like to meet Janice and Big Jim someday." Then he sighed dramatically. "But I suppose I never will. After all, people like them NEVER come to my office. The only people I ever meet are crazies, like you."

John laughed. Dr. Chester then added, "But I mistake in saying that. I don't think you're in that category. In fact, it seems clear now that you never were." He paused for a moment, looking at John curiously. "I have just one last question for you, my boy. Do you ever feel gay cravings? Does it sometimes come back to you? Has it completely disappeared? Do you think it could return someday?"

John smiled and shook his head. "No," he said simply. "It could never return. That would require me to engage in too many lies to myself. I could never live that untruthfully with myself again."

John walked over to stare absently at one of the pictures on the wall of the Doctor's office. It showed a sunset, or sunrise--it was hard to tell which. "As for your other question about cravings," said John, "Big Jim explained that to me too. When I was with him in the mountains and began to see the truth about my gayness and that I wasn't gay after all, I was surprised sometimes when I felt some of the old cravings coming back, kind of out of the blue. It made me wonder if maybe my new thinking wasn't correct, and that I had some inner gayness that could not be pulled out no matter what I did."

John turned to look at the Doctor who was still nonsensically munching on his chicken foot. "But when I asked Jim about it, he said there's nothing unusual about that at all. Any addictive behavior we have indulged in that involves our bodies will sometimes hit us with cravings at unexpected times. That's perfectly normal. We see it all the time with smokers and drinkers, and drug addicts. Just because a craving comes doesn't mean the addiction is inherent or unavoidable, but only that we have to re-assert our power over it."

"Jim said it was like pounding a nail into a board, and later pulling out the nail. When you do, a hole is left behind. You can fill up the hole and paint over it and make it disappear, but in reality the hole is still there, and if you hit just the right spot the filler will come out causing the hole to become visible again. It's like that with addictions. They create a small trouble spot ever after by leaving a hole behind that could always flare up into a problem unless a person is constantly and persistently vigilant."

"Occasional thoughts or cravings do not mean the addiction has not been completely overcome, or that a person is doomed to be a slave to that addiction forever. What it does mean however is that the person has to reaffirm that he is stronger than the addiction and has overcome it, and will fulfill the promise they made to themselves to NEVER indulge in it again no matter what. We see this in people who overcome smoking all the time. It's the same with gayness. When we reaffirm again and again that it has been overcome and that we control it, rather than it controlling us, this just shows that this 'weakness' has become strong to us. And with each reaffirmation, we become a little bit stronger and the weakness a little weaker. Of course, it would have been better to never have indulged in the addiction to begin with, which created an occasional craving we have to deal with for a long time afterward. But with time the cravings come less and less, and eventually they disappear completely."

Dr. Chester stopped nibbling on his chicken foot and smiled at John. Then he rose from his couch and assumed the most pompous stance he could muster. The effort was ruined, of course, by the wobbly chicken foot he still held in his hand.

"My boy," said Dr. Chester dramatically, "after all that has been covered in our many discussions, it is my professional opinion that you are not gay. It no longer has the hold on you that it once did."

John smiled. "It never really had any hold, did it? Only what I gave it. And once I realized that fact and changed my thinking, it quickly disappeared. It was always an illusion."

Dr. Chester came over and extended his hand toward John--the hand without the chicken foot. "Go out and conquer the world,

John." He said simply. "There's nothing holding you back."

John shook the doctor's hand so vigorously that the chicken foot in the other hand wobbled. "That's just what Janice and I are going to do. And we're going to start by going up in the mountains this weekend to visit Big Jim, Rainy and Benjy. Janice is very anxious to meet them, she's heard me talk so much about them."

Dr. Chester raised an eyebrow. "So you've told her all about your past then? All the details? The gayness and everything?"

"Yes," said John simply. "Janice is not someone you play games with, or hide things from. And she understands. She's ok with it all because as she says, the past doesn't hold us hostage unless we let it. We can forgive and move on. We live in today, not yesterday."

"Very profound," said Dr. Chester again. "I'll let your grandfather know that I believe further visits between us are unnecessary. He's being paying the bills for your visits, you know.

Otherwise I would now have the pleasure of demanding full payment of my exorbitant fee from you!" He sighed with a sudden frown. "It's very sad, really. Just think of all the money I was getting because of you, which I will no longer be getting ..."

John just laughed, then sauntered out of the office. Dr. Chester watched through his window as his ex-patient emerged from the building and went out to the Mazda in the parking lot. The smile John flashed at Janice was as fresh and clean and untroubled as that of a newborn baby.

Dr. Chester looked down suddenly at the chicken foot still in his hand. "You know," he said softly, "someone needs to teach the Brazilians there are better parts of the chicken to eat than this."

November 15, 2016

Mr. Frederick Anderson
2974 Lerue Lane

San Francisco, CA

Dear Mr. Anderson,

Your grandson and I had our last session today in my office. Things went as I had hoped, and in some ways even better. John now has a girlfriend named Janice who was waiting for him in the parking lot. From the way he described her she seems like a very sensible girl, who is not troubled by John's past. She also has extremely wise ideas about sexual abstinence and purity. She seems to inherently know that promiscuity is harmful to individuals, and that the most complete sexual satisfaction can only be found after the commitment of marriage has occurred. You don't find too many girls with such sensible ideas anymore.

As I indicated in my last letter, I am of the professional opinion that John has overcome the notions of gayness that he once possessed. He probably does not realize it, but his success in doing so has come from within himself. He ascribes most of it to Big Jim and God of course, but if you were to ask the mountain man the truth I am sure he would say he had only a small part in it. Like all patients who attain healing, both physical and mental, the process is internal. All anyone on the outside can do is to present true and correct ideas, and then give unconditional and sincere love and encouragement. The patient must do the rest themselves.

Which now takes us to you, as John's grandfather. In our last meeting John described the wonders of the principle of forgiveness that he learned from Big Jim. I hope you will not take offense if I now direct that idea toward you. You need to apply the principle of forgiveness yourself in all your future interactions with John. Forget his past and accept him as he is. That is exactly what Janice has done, and it seems to be working wonderfully well for her. As you do this you will create a positive and pleasant bond between yourself and John that will last a lifetime.

Most importantly, remember that your love and goodwill toward John need to be unconditional. You love him simply because he IS, just like Big Jim loved him when they first met, even though John was still convinced he was gay, and certainly looked and acted that way. It was that love and unconditional acceptance by Jim which I believe was the strongest motivation for John to overcome his gayness. When he saw that he was worthwhile and lovable regardless of anything, he began to respond to Jim's kindness and good view of his potential. This led to a willingness to listen to Jim's ideas, and ultimately to accept what Jim told him about gayness. Remember that unconditional love does not mean acceptance or approval of a lifestyle you do not agree with. It is simply loving people regardless, nothing more, nothing less. Like Big Jim, I am sure you can find a way to do this that does not compromise your own personal standards.

My final bill is attached to this letter. Thank you for your prompt payments, since as I have said before I like money. I would be happy to meet with you for lunch sometime, if you wish. I won't even charge you my hourly rate! We could meet at 'Lilly's Limpid Liquid Limelunchery' where I hear they have a most impressive root beer and catsup float.

Best wishes,

Franklin Chester, PhD

OTHER BOOKS BY THE AUTHOR

<u>Nonfiction</u>

<u>The Ninth Amendment: Key to Understanding the Bill of Rights</u>. This book explains how the Ninth Amendment is the key to understanding rights in the United States. The founders created the Ninth Amendment to protect unlisted natural law rights as they were understood in their day. This amendment was never intended to allow future generations to create new rights. Rather, it was to safeguard the morality and natural rights of the founding generation.

<u>Judicial Activism: A Way to Overcome It</u>. Judicial activism in the U.S. occurs when a few Supreme Court judges decide public policy issues, which normally deal with rights. However, it would be better for the people to decide such issues through their elected representatives. This book proposes a way to remove judicial activism, by returning to an original view of the founding fathers that preferred legislative oversight of rights issues.

<u>Rights in America, Bills of Attainder and the Ninth Amendment</u>. While rights in America have always been cherished, many people today misunderstand the source of their rights. They have come to believe that government is the grantor of rights. The flipside of this belief is that

government can also take them away. Such a view conflicts with that of the founders, who gave us the ban on bills of attainder and 9th Amendment to forever protect our natural rights.

Our Sex Saturated Society. American society is obsessed with sex. This obsession has led to extreme results that would be considered appalling by prior generations, such as: rampant premarital sex which increases AIDS while decreasing trust and commitment between partners; gays/lesbians elevating sex to such an extreme it has become their god; and abortions in which innocent unborns are yanked out piece by piece.

False Worlds. A false world is like an apple full of worms. It appears juicy and attractive on the outside, but is in fact disgusting on the inside. This book discusses a number of false worlds masquerading as truth but which are in fact false to their core. Included are the false worlds of politics, international relations, law, sexual confusion (premarital sex, abortion and gayness), entertainment and pride.

The Anti Stupidity Book. Stupidity. What is it? Is it just something we see our neighbors and members of the opposite political party do? Or is it something more? Why does it seem to be so universal? Are there fundamentals of stupidity that can be recognized? These are the questions discussed in this book. It presents six fundamentals of stupidity that lead to the stupid choices that we see all around us. Included among these are the belief that there are no moral values, that God does not exist, and that it is acceptable to become addicted and to treat others badly and be proud. In the end we see that the only sure way to avoid the fundamentals of stupidity is through the saving power of Jesus Christ.

Adult Fiction

Miss Lydia Fairbanks and the Losers Club. Miss Lydia Fairbanks is the newest teacher at Inner City Junior High School, the deadliest school in the state. While the school principal believes she won't last a day, Miss Fairbanks quickly surprises everyone by not only surviving in the midst of her killer students, but actually thriving in the classroom. But even someone as weak and small as Miss Fairbanks can harbor secrets from the past ...

Crazy Pete. On a dark night in a lonely park in LA, crazy old Pete saves a teenager named Kelly from a suicidal encounter with a street gang. While Kelly initially resists Pete's kindness, he is gradually drawn into the life and service of his unusual mentor--a lifestyle of total concentration on others, and forgetting of himself. But even Crazy Pete has secrets, and one day, with a shock, the boy learns the terrible history of Pete's past that turned him into the saint he has become.

My Name is Kate and I Just Killed My Baby. Kate's journal begins with a very simple entry. "I like pizza and ice cream and going on dates and watching funny movies. I like to swim and text on my phone and go skiing in the winter. Oh, and there's one more thing you should know about me. I just killed my baby." Join Kate as she struggles with the aftermath of having an abortion, and the nightmare she never dreamed would follow.

Running for the Guv. Blake Guv is a starving young attorney fresh out of law school, desperately trying to get new clients. In a mad gamble to obtain some publicity he foolishly enters the race for Governor of his state as an independent candidate. But when a series of unexpected events shove him to the front of the race, Blake is appalled at the prospect he just might win--since he hates politics with a passion!

Santa v Afton. Shortly before Christmas the tiny town of Afton is shocked when everyone is sued by a man claiming to be Santa Claus. His lawsuit is for wrongfully 'firing' him from his delivery job, since he can only come to people who believe. With less than two weeks until Christmas, will Santa's lawsuit convince them to change their minds?

Juvenile Fiction

My Science Teacher is a Wizard. Fifth grader Blake Drywater has a new wizard science teacher, who promptly turns Blake's class into roaches and earthworms. But Blake soon learns there is more than science going on in his classroom. An evil wizard is seeking a powerful potion his teacher has made. And when Blake is given the potion soon thereafter, he finds himself facing problems far harder than any science exam! Book 1 of 'The Stewards of Light' series.

My Math Teacher is a Vampire. Blake Drywater and his fellow unfortunate students at Millard Fillmore Middle School once more find themselves facing an unexpected creature in one of their classes. Because of a sudden 'neck disorder' suffered by their math teacher, Blake and his classmates receive a chilling substitute. His name is Mr. Coagulate, who has a strange fascination with blood and dreams. Book 2 of 'The Stewards of Light' series.

My History Teacher is a Leprechaun. Blake Drywater has a new history teacher--a leprechaun who escorts Blake to the underground time tunnels of his people. These tunnels are full of doors that open to different places and times, including the future. But then Blake discovers the real reason for his visit, and how it just might destroy the world!

Detectives in Diapers: They Mystery of the Aztec Amulet. Flo and Mo are not ordinary babies. Although they are only fourteen months old, they can use a computer, trick any mindless adult they want, and help their goofy detective father solve baffling crimes. Then a mysterious girl comes to their father, claiming that her grandmother has disappeared. Will the babies' superior brains be able to solve the mystery and save their bumbling parents?

Cloud Trouble. Inventor Uncle Ned has discovered that clouds are alive and can be transformed into common objects. He gives his nephew Talmage a cloud turned into a pen, with the assignment to see what it says and does. However, Talmage soon learns that THIS cloud is nothing but trouble since it insults everyone they meet! And since no one believes pens can talk, they think Talmage is the one saying the insults!

ABOUT THE AUTHOR

Duane L. Ostler was raised in Southern Idaho, where the wind never stops. He has lived in Australia, Mexico, Brazil, China, the big Island of Hawaii, and—most foreign of all—New Jersey. He has driven an ice cream truck, sold auto parts, been a tax collector, and sued people as an attorney. He has also obtained a PhD in law. He and his wife have five children and two cats. If you would like to contact Mr. Ostler you can reach him at: duanelostler@gmail.com

Made in the USA
Las Vegas, NV
23 February 2022

44420903R00089